DUNLEARY

DUNLEARY

Monica Heath

CHIVERS
THORNDIKE

This Large Print edition is published by BBC Audiobooks Ltd, Bath, England and by Thorndike Press, Waterville, Maine, USA.

Published in 2004 in the U.K. by arrangement with the Author.

Published in 2004 in the U.S. by arrangement with Maureen Moran Agency.

U.K. Hardcover ISBN 0–7540–9917–2 (Chivers Large Print)
U.S. Softcover   ISBN 0–7862–6278–8 (General)

The text of this Large Print edition is unabridged.
Other aspects of the book may vary from the original edition.

Set in 16 pt. New Times Roman.

Printed in Great Britain on acid-free paper.

British Library Cataloguing in Publication Data available

Library of Congress Control Number: 2003115691

CHAPTER ONE

It seemed incredible to me when I first came to Dunleary, that I, who had never known the sea, should find myself suddenly set down in the midst of it, never out of sight nor sound of its cruel lashings and pummelings, and I found myself pausing often to listen to the surf striking the cliffs below the castle. There was something sinister in the sound, and savage.

I had come to Dunleary filled with a number of hopes and expectations, for I had married the King of *Inish Laoghaire*, which is Irish for Leary Island, the detached bit of stone off the west coat of Ireland, on which Dunleary stands.

Then suddenly my hopes were shattered, for I found myself married to a stranger, and afraid.

* * *

Count Saint Brendan O'Leary first came into my life the night of my cousin Catherine's debut, which was held at San Francisco's St. Maurice Yacht club, on the Marina. I was being presented with Catherine, though I shouldn't have been there at all had it not been for my uncle Connary Rynne, who was a wealthy man, and I a poor relation he had taken in.

The first of the guests had begun to arrive, the women hurrying forward to shower Catherine with tinkling librettos of affection, the men bending gallantly over my cousin's upturned face to kiss her. I glimpsed curiosity in their eyes, when they turned to me, and I felt exposed and uncomfortable in the midst of all of the excitement and glamor, which seemed suddenly rather false. Unexpectedly, I found myself visualizing the cool, dense, Ohio woods, where, as a child, I had run to hide, and I closed my eyes against the brightness and gaiety.

When I opened my eyes again, he was there, standing beneath the Boldocchi arch that framed the lounge doorway, a tall, dark-haired stranger, watching me with a peculiar little smile lifting brows that were very black and rakish against his weathered face. I guessed that he had caught me staring at him, and I felt suddenly foolish.

The stranger paused for an instant, the ferns and scarlet roses of the arch fluting romantically about his dark head. His eyes were level beneath his odd, swooping brows, and very bright. A smile that seemed a strange mixture of condescension and patient endurance lifted the corners of his full, sensuous mouth as he swept the room with his penetrating gaze. There was an unmistakable air of arrogance about him.

2

His gaze came back to me, and I fancied, with a little start, that I glimpsed wickedness in him. The thought amazed me.

'He's come, after all!' Catherine said, beside me.

'Who is he?' I asked.

'The O'Leary,' Catherine said, with a pleased laugh. 'Count Brendan O'Leary, to be precise, from the castle Dunleary, in Ireland.'

'But they don't have counts in Ireland,' I blurted. 'They've only earls and lords, like the English.'

'Really, Deirdre,' Catherine scolded, her laughter tinged with subtle scorn. 'Must you be gauche?'

She told me then that she had happened into my uncle's office a few days earlier, and had discovered the Count there discussing business of some sort with Uncle Con.

'He just happened to mention that he would be staying on in San Francisco for an indefinite length of time,' Catherine added, innocently. 'And I insisted, of course that Father send him an invitation to the ball.' She lifted her bouquet of Camelot roses to shield her ripe, red lips.

'I had heard of him before, of course,' she continued, still speaking behind her flowers, her brown eyes alive with interest. 'In fact, his name is quite well known in our social circle, though he seldom puts in an appearance at any of the exciting places. But it really doesn't

3

matter,' she said. 'The point is, this fabulous Irish male never, but never, condescends to show himself. You can imagine how stunned I was to discover him there in Father's office. How he managed to tear himself away from his dreary old castle remains a mystery.

'According to Father, Dunleary is a moldering old place, sitting high on some naked little island off the coast of Ireland. As isolated as some ruinous old monastery. There's some hideous legend connected with it, though Father refused to tell me what it is, poor thing. His face grew absolutely livid when I asked, and he mumbled something about it being a story unfit for his daughter's ears.'

Catherine grew silent, then, her throat trembling with a strange laugh, as Count O'Leary left his place beneath the arch to make his way toward us. The hint of wickedness still lurked in his eyes, which, I saw, as he drew near, were a wonderful, sunlit shade of brown. I fancied that I caught a glow of triumph in their clear depths.

Uncle Con appeared to introduce us, and Count O'Leary reached for my gloved hand, repeating my name after my uncle in a softly resonant voice.

'Deirdre Rynne.' He flashed me a warm smile. 'Deirdre *ni* Rynne.' He repeated it a second time, in a voice suddenly rich with brogue.

Then, quite unexpectedly, he leaned

4

forward and kissed me very gently on the cheek.

Flustered, I lowered my eyes, focusing my gaze on the immense, crested ring that gleamed against his hand, casting about desperately for some devastatingly clever little remark.

'Thank you,' I heard myself saying, and I knew, the instant that I said it, that I had committed a hopeless faux pas.

Count O'Leary's eyes, shot through with specks of green and gold fire, gleamed with amusement. 'Your gratitude tempts me to do a better job of it, Deirdre *ni* Rynne,' he said. 'And I promise you that next time, I shall,' he added softly, his eyes flashing wickedly in his tan face.

I knew then that I had been right about his having a cruel streak. Blushing furiously, I turned from him, barely controlling a desire to bolt from the room.

He had turned to Catherine, and, as he did so, a startling change came over him. His lips closed in upon themselves, becoming deceptively thin-lined and grim. The warm specks of light disappeared from his eyes, leaving them cool and distant. My cousin looked up at him, an expression of dismay on her clever, heart-shaped face.

'So nice to see you again, Count,' she said, in a sharp voice, giving a fiery toss of her head that sent her black hair dancing along her bare

5

shoulders.

'My pleasure, I'm sure,' he countered in a stiff, wary voice.

He turned very quickly, and disappeared into the crowd, leaving Catherine speechless in his wake.

Later, I caught him watching her, an angry expression on his handsome face. Catherine, feeling this, turned to him, tossing her head charmingly in his direction, emitting a taunting little laugh that tinkled across the room, causing people to turn and stare. Count O'Leary switched his gaze at once to me.

'Damn him,' Catherine hissed, her face going very white.

'He's made you angry,' I said, thinking how stunning she looked, her pale face contrasting sharply with her jet hair and her low-cut, ruby gown.

It occurred to me how Spanish she looked, and I guessed that her striking, Latin beauty had somehow intimidated the handsome Irish count. There seemed, at the time, to be no better explanation for his aloof behavior.

'If only Angelina would arrive,' Catherine said. 'I can't imagine what is keeping her.'

The Condesa Angelina de Gomez, who was my cousin's best friend, was flying in from the Argentine to stand beside Catherine in the receiving line. The Condesa had wired that afternoon to say that she would be late.

Now, glancing at my watch, which was a gift

6

from Uncle Con, I reminded Catherine of this. She laughed suddenly, in the rather sharp way she had when she was irritated with someone—humorless laughter.

'You've worn that watch with your party dress,' she said, reminding me of my awkwardness. 'Really, it's hardly suitable.'

I had never worn a party dress before. I had always been painfully plain, and even had my parents been able to afford it, I was hardly the type for long gowns and frills. Freckles, a discouraging number of them, spattered my face and arms and legs. I had never tried to combat them, as some girls did, perhaps because Mother had been freckled, and on her I had found them quite pleasing. But Mother was gone, now. And Father. I had entered a new world when I came to live with Uncle Con, one where appearances seemed to matter a good deal.

I wished, as I stood next to Catherine's sleek beauty, that I had known better than to wear the watch.

Then suddenly, the Condesa was announced, and Catherine left the receiving line, rushing forward with great eagerness to receive her embrace. The two of them were shockingly alike. I must have gasped my surprise, for Aunt Ruth said in a low voice, 'Quite startling, isn't it?'

'I hadn't realized before just how Spanish Catherine is,' I murmured.

Aunt Ruth said, 'Catherine hasn't always been the girl you see now, dear. Your cousin has created her own image, patterning herself after the Condesa. And the Condesa's daughter,' she added. 'Her name was Katherine, with a K, though they called her Katsy. After Catherine's transformation, the two of them were enough alike to pass for twins.'

'I'm afraid I don't understand,' I said.

'It's quite simple, dear. Catherine dyed her hair that intense shade of black, and tinted her brows. Even her widow's peak, so like the Condesa's, is contrived. I must admit that the result is totally devastating. Even though Catherine is no longer her own person,' Aunt Ruth added, with a sad little sigh.

'I can't imagine why she should have wanted to change herself,' I said, remembering that Aunt Ruth was Catherine's stepmother, and wondering if perhaps that were the reason.

'Perhaps because her mother is dead, and the Condesa, being her godmother, is the next best thing,' Aunt Ruth said. 'You know, dear, that Catherine spends all of her summers in the Argentine, at the De Gomez villa, or in Spain, at some old castle that has been in the Condesa's family for centuries. It must all seem terribly romantic to an impressionable young girl.'

'Will the Condesa's daughter be here tonight?' I asked, my curiosity aroused.

'I'm afraid not,' Aunt Ruth said. 'The Condesa's daughter is no longer living.'

I wanted to ask what had happened to the girl, but Aunt Ruth had turned away from me to speak to a friend.

I stood watching my cousin and the handsome Argentine woman make their way toward us, seeing Catherine lean close to whisper something in the Condesa's ear. Angelina de Gomez turned rather abruptly, then, to glance at Count O'Leary.

Then a queer thing happened. The Condesa de Gomez turned suddenly pale, and one of her slim hands flew frantically to clutch at the slender column of her throat. There was a certain desperation in the gesture, and I found myself thinking that she would faint.

However, she regained her composure almost immediately, and she and Catherine joined Aunt Ruth and me as though nothing out of the ordinary had happened.

'What is it, Angelina?' Aunt Ruth fussed over her, a worried expression on her kind face. 'If you are ill, dear, please don't feel that you must . . .'

The Condesa smiled graciously, interrupting Aunt Ruth with a charming gesture. '*Verdaderamente*, it is nothing,' she said. 'A touch of migraine. I've been plagued with them all of my life. The pain has passed, now. I shall be quite all right, I assure you.'

She received with us, then, her eyes flashing

from time to time in Count O'Leary's direction. I fancied that I detected a glimmer of fear in their dark depths and I guessed that it had not been a migraine, after all, that had caused her to go pale and clutch so helplessly at her remarkably white throat.

*   *   *

We danced that evening in the club's Ponce de León Room, which was spaciously Spanish, with polished suits of armor arranged against startlingly lifelike murals of the conquistadors. A glittering 'Fountain of Youth,' flooded with prisms of light, sparkled at the room's center. I felt awed by it all, and a little frightened.

When Breck Panaker, who was my escort, for the evening—one of the airline Panakers, Catherine had told me—took me into his arms to lead off the dancing, I followed his gliding feet as best I could, fully aware, once more, of my awkwardness. I wished with a passion that I might escape him.

I kept taking uneasy glances over Breck's shoulder, as we danced, hoping for some glimpse of Count O'Leary. I failed to locate him, and I wondered if he had found the cotillion dull, and had already gone.

The oddly expectant smile the Count had flashed at me in the club lounge still haunted me. Who was he, and why had he looked at me in just that way, I wondered. What was more, why had he seemed rude to Catherine, who was far lovelier than I could ever hope to be, and what had made the Condesa de Gomez so obviously fear him?

Perhaps because my mind had wandered from the dancing, the toe of my slipper caught in the hem of my long gown, and even before I glanced down and saw the slit in the blue satin, I knew that it was torn. I looked up helplessly at Breck Panaker, tears of embarrassment gathering in my eyes.

I swallowed the harsh lump in my throat, determined not to embarrass Aunt Ruth and Uncle Con.

'I'm sorry,' I said to Breck. 'But I simply can't go on. As you can see, it presents a hazard.' I stuck the pointed toe of my slipper through the torn cloth, borrowing a little laugh from Catherine to cover my frustration.

'It's only a dress,' Breck Panaker said, giving me a patient smile.

'Obviously, I'll have to retire to the powder room for repairs,' I said.

I fancied that Breck seemed relieved.

*   *   *

A black-uniformed maid sat in one corner of the powder room, reading a magazine. She seemed unsympathetic when I showed her my gown. When I offered to repair the rent myself, she flashed me a suspicious look, and,

11

refusing to yield her needle to me, jabbed it viciously into the soft cloth. I escaped from her as quickly as I could, longing suddenly for some quiet corner where I might be alone for a while, to regain my courage.

One of the doors which opened off the broad, deeply carpeted hallway stood ajar, and I peeked beyond its thick panels, glimpsing book-lined walls. The room seemed empty, and I dared to venture inside.

I scanned the bookshelves eagerly, for good books had always been one of my weaknesses. A slim volume bound in expensive, mottled calfskin caught my eye, and I went to take it down. Surprisingly, it was a book of Yeats, my mother's favorite among the Irish poets.

A sudden, poignant longing sprang up in me, and I went to one of the deep chairs, where I sat, gently turning the thin pages, hearing suddenly my mother's soft voice.

I became aware of footsteps and realized that someone else had entered the room.

'It's an extremely small world, Condesa,' a man's voice said, behind me. I recognized it, at once, as Count O'Leary's. 'You are, of course, the last person I expected to meet here tonight.'

I caught the rustle of silks and knew that the Condesa de Gomez had entered the room with him.

'What are you doing here?' she demanded regally.

A chill swept through me, and I imagined, for a frightening instant, that my presence had been detected. Then Count O'Leary's voice sounded once more, and I knew that I hadn't been seen.

'I might ask the same thing of you, Condesa,' he said.

'I am Catherine Rynne's godmother,' the Condesa stated. 'Who has a better right than I to be here? I was her mother's friend for years. Yet, I've not the slightest recollection of having ever heard your name mentioned in the Rynne household.'

'I'm not a friend of the family, if that is what is bothering you, Condesa,' Count O'Leary said, sounding faintly amused. 'It is merest chance that brought me here tonight. A most fortunate quirk of fate.'

'I believe that fate can be extremely callous and cruel,' the Condesa said, in a trembling voice.

'I beg to differ,' Count O'Leary said. 'It was hardly fate that brought your daughter to Dunleary, Condesa. We are both aware, I am sure, that she came of her own free will, deliberately, and for her own peculiar reasons. That she never left my island . . .'

'Was hardly fate, either,' the Condesa broke in, her voice becoming harsh. 'You must know that I've never been satisfied with the explanation I received of Katsy's death.'

'In other words, you believe that we

13

O'Learys are murderers,' Count O'Leary snapped.

There was a brief silence, charged with tension, during which I found myself trembling with fear.

'Please,' the Condesa's voice became pleading. 'I . . . It's only that I can't imagine her dead. I've even suspected that she might not be; that she is simply hiding away somewhere, to punish me. You must know the sort of girl she was.'

'Very well,' Count O'Leary said, in a voice tinged with bitterness.

'If your being here tonight has something to do with my goddaughter, Catherine Rynne, I must warn you that I shall expose you to her father.' The Condesa's voice became suddenly haughty. 'Connary Rynne is a wealthy man, as you know, with a good deal of influence. If it should happen that you are concealing Katsy—aiding her in some horrible scheme . . .'

'There is nothing to reveal,' Count O'Leary said. 'Your daughter came to my island of her own free will. She met with an accident. What more can I say?

'Perhaps it will ease your mind, Condesa,' he continued, 'to know that I thoroughly distrust the virtue of brightly painted flowers.' His voice was slightly mocking. 'However, I must admit that your goddaughter has accomplished a remarkable resemblance with her little artifices. I find it rather difficult, in

14

fact, to keep it straight in my mind just who she is.'

'You came to dislike my daughter,' the Condesa said. 'And now that she is gone, I am forced to take comfort in my godchild.'

My breath caught in my throat. Was he a murderer? Had Count Brendan O'Leary killed Katsy de Gomez? Or was she simply hiding somewhere, as the Condesa seemed to suspect?

'You needn't worry. I've a keenness for freckled faces and sandy hair,' Count O'Leary was saying.

'Are you trying to tell me that your being here has something to do with that plain little fledgling Connary has taken in? Deirdre, isn't it? Deirdre Rynne. How appropriate the name is to her!' The Condesa emitted a brittle laugh. 'Even Ruth's clever efforts have failed to turn her into anything.'

'Somehow, her innocence has remained undefiled, thanks be to God,' Count O'Leary said.

'You sound actually smitten,' the Condesa de Gomez said. 'And a little mad,' she added, with at touch of malice.

'Mad or not, I fully intend to claim her,' Count O'Leary said in a low voice. 'I've come to take her back with me, to Ireland.'

They left then, and I sat numbly, the Count's strange words ringing ominously in my ears.

* * *

Count O'Leary stood outside the ballroom door when I returned, leaning casually against the arched frame, watching the dancers revolving inside. I felt his touch on my arm.

'Deirdre,' he said. 'Deirdre *ni* Rynne.' He lifted his devilish brows. 'Are you idle, by chance?' he asked then, his fingers burning into my bare flesh.

A feeling of guilt surged up in me, coupled with a nameless fear. I fancied that he could see into me and knew that I had been concealed there in the club library, listening shamelessly to his conversation.

'Idle?' I said, my face flaming.

His eyes filled with mischief. 'That happens to be the way we ask a girl to dance in Ireland,' he explained.

'My parents came from Ireland,' I blurted irrelevantly, overcome with relief.

'We should get on famously then,' he said.

Drawing me into his arms, he guided me effortlessly through the doorway, onto the ballroom floor, his luminous eyes never leaving my face. It occurred to me that he was perhaps as fascinated with me as I had become with him, and I felt hopelessly flattered. I relaxed, thinking: He can't simply waft me away, not with all of these people about.

Catherine danced by in Breck Panaker's

16

arms, flashing me a disbelieving look. She gave one of her peculiar laughs, and I imagined that it sounded bitter.

An instant change came over Count O'Leary at the sight of her. His feet faltered for the barest instant.

'If one didn't know,' I ventured, 'one might never guess that Catherine is at least half Irish. She looks so exquisitely Spanish.'

'I've no taste for Latin women, contrived or otherwise,' Count O'Leary said shortly. 'I much prefer them tawny. Like you,' he added, his voice softening.

I said, 'That is the first time anyone ever referred to me as tawny. I must say, it sounds rather wicked. Like some lithe, stalking jungle cat, intent on seeking her prey. However, I'm afraid that I'm not at all like that, though it sounds terribly romantic.'

'You've no sly little scheme, then, to catch a man?'

I glanced up quickly to see if he were laughing at me. His face seemed entirely serious.

'No,' I said. 'It never occurred to me that I might be successful.'

'That means that you are free and unattached,' he stated in a pleased voice.

I nodded.

'You may as well know that I'm keen for tawny girls. With freckles,' he added. 'Particularly with freckles.' He laid an accusing finger on the tip of my nose.

'Aunt Ruth's camouflage hasn't worked, then,' I said. 'Not that I'm disappointed. I hardly approved of it in the first place.'

'Then why did you submit?' he demanded.

'Because I felt I owed it to Uncle Con,' I said. 'My parents are both gone, and he has done a good deal for me.'

'That's no excuse to betray yourself,' he stated. 'If your uncle hadn't liked you just as you were, he'd hardly have taken an interest.' He paused, his gold-flecked eyes quickly scanning my face. 'I should like very much to see your freckles,' he said then. 'I should like very much to see you with your face scrubbed free of all that paint, and your hair hanging free to catch the sun and blowing a little in the breeze.'

He pulled me very close, and laid his cheek against the top of my head. I sensed that something about me excited him tremendously, and a feeling of delight came over me.

We danced near to the ballroom door, and he held me away for a moment, asking if I would care to step out for a breath of air. The ballroom had become very close.

I hesitated, recalling the conversation I had overheard.

'Are you afraid of me?' he demanded, with uncanny insight.

'No,' I said, as calmly as I could. 'It's just that it's always rather cool here on the bay at night, Count O'Leary. There is invariably a brisk wind blowing in off the water.'

'You must call me Bren,' he said. 'And I shall call you Deirdre. What's more, I promise that I shan't permit you to freeze so much as your little finger.'

He was teasing again, his eyes burning down at me from beneath their satanical brows, aflame with mischief. I felt suddenly foolish, telling myself that I had been too deeply affected by the romantic lights of the fountain.

CHAPTER TWO

It was a delightfully clear night. In the distance, the Richmond lights danced like fireflies against the Contra Costa hills.

Bren O'Leary placed the soft, white cashmere wrap Aunt Ruth had purchased to go with my gown snugly about my shoulders. He had retrieved a black topcoat for himself. It made him seem taller than before—dark and villainous and terribly attractive. I found myself responding to him. I allowed him to slip his arm about me, and we strolled, our bodies touching, out onto the pier, between the rows of dancing boats.

When we reached the far end, he leaned back casually against the rail, to light a cigarette. The flame from his lighter illuminated his face, casting an orange glow across its smooth planes, emphasizing the devilish swoop of his dark brows.

'I've come a long way to find a girl with freckles,' he said, his voice softly vibrant. Passionate, I thought, with a twinge of alarm.

'There must be any number of turkey-egg girls in Ireland, if it's freckles you want,' I protested, giving a panicky little laugh. 'Though I suspect that most men prefer a flawless, soap-ad skin. You must be the exception,' I rattled on clumsily.

'Every man has his own personal concept of a girl,' he said. 'It happens that you fit mine.'

His soft voice lulled me. I felt drawn to it against my will. It occurred to me that I was as naive as a child, that I hadn't the least idea what a man like this might expect of a woman who interested him. Had he been serious, in what he had said to the Condesa, about claiming me?

I said, 'I've had little experience with clever repartee. I fear that I am the sort of girl who might take you quite seriously. You see, I really haven't known many men. None at all, in fact, other than Father and Uncle Con.'

I turned from him, gazing wistfully across the dark water.

'I didn't expect that you had,' he said. 'And it is my intention that you should take what I say quite seriously.'

His arms came about me, pulling me to face

him. I tried to read his face in the faint glow cast by the harbor lights, not quite trusting him.

'Perhaps I should be getting back inside,' I said. 'Aunt Ruth will miss me and worry.'

'You *are* frightened of me,' he said.

'Yes,' I admitted. 'I think I am, just a little.'

'How old are you?' he demanded.

'Nineteen,' I told him.

'It's time, then, that a man talked to you like this, Roisin,' he said.

'My mother used to call me that,' I told him, a catch coming into my voice. 'Roisin. Little Rose.'

The same haunting nostalgia that I had experienced in the club library when I discovered the Yeats swept through me, shattering my defenses. My mother and father had been gone less than three months. They were still very much in my mind.

'You said she was dead, Roisin,' Bren whispered, against my hair. 'I'm sorry.' His arms tightened, almost imperceptibly.

I thought: He, too, has suffered some unbearable loss in his life, and knows exactly how I feel. It was hardly more than a fleeting impression, but because of it, I let him comfort me, forgetting that I had glimpsed cruelty in him and that he had seemed perhaps a bit forward in the things he had said.

'She used to tell me about the little people,' I said. 'She told me that they live in mounds,

21

and beneath the rocks. Sometimes, when I am feeling blue, I pretend that I am still a child, and I find myself slipping away to the Japanese Tea Garden in the park, where there are any number of quite likely-seeming stones.' Then, realizing that I must seem hopelessly sentimental, I forced a small laugh. 'It's the nearest thing I've found, in San Francisco, to their natural habitat. And watching for fairies really makes quite a delightful afternoon.'

'What else did your mother tell you about the homeland?' he asked. There was an unmistakable eagerness in his voice. I fancied that I felt a throbbing through his dark coat, as though his heart had speeded with anticipation.

'She always called it that,' I said. 'The homeland. "My heart is in the homeland," she used to say to me, when she felt discouraged. She had leukemia, you know'—though, of course, he couldn't possibly. 'It was only a matter of time . . .' My voice dwindled off as the pain came flooding back.

'And you nursed her,' Bren said.

I nodded. 'She was an excellent patient. She never complained.' My eyes blurred unexpectedly with tears, thinking of her.

I saw Mother, her eyes fox-colored and as warm as flames. Everything about Mother had been warm—her shining hair, which she wore twined into a thick braid. Without her, I thought, it had been as though the sunlight

22

had been turned off. Father had met her, one summer, at the state fair, and Mother always said he had been attracted to her because she was Irish, like himself.

The Rynnes had been famine Irish, Father once told me. To escape the poverty of the homeland, he and Uncle Con had migrated to America. When Father married Mother, the two brothers had parted. They had never seen each other again. The only times Father mentioned Uncle Con were when he had been drinking. I remembered one time in particular, when Father had let it slip that Uncle Con had suspected Mother of having an indiscreet past—something that she wanted to keep hidden. For this, Father could never forgive him.

Father had his own peculiarities, although as a child I was never fully aware of them. It was only after I had grown older that I came to realize that Father was a drifter. He wandered about rather aimlessly from job to job, taking us with him. I couldn't remember a time when he hadn't been overly fond of the bottle.

Mother scolded him at times about his drinking. But even I could see that her heart wasn't in it. A sort of sadness would come over her when Father appeared at his worst, as though it pained her to know that he needed something more than she was able to give him.

I remembered days when Mother had seemed deceptively well, and I was deluded into thinking that her condition had improved. Father shared my hopefulness those times, and stayed sober, so that it seemed that each of us had taken a new lease on life, and nothing could ever again frighten us.

Recklessly, Father would neglect his job at the steel mill, or wherever he happened to be working at the time, to be with her, and the three of us would go out into the country and roam the woods, Father carrying Mother, who was as light as a feather. We lived in Licking County for a time, near the Ohio earthworks and historical mounds that always reminded Mother of the faery dwellings in her beloved homeland and, to please her, Father would recite wild tales of the little people in his booming voice.

There had been one time in particular that I had never forgotten. It was the only time that Mother, seeming to forget herself, had mentioned something personal in connection with the homeland.

'My father rode his horses over them in Ireland,' she had said of the fairy mounds. Raths, she called them. The fairy forts.

When I asked her about the man who had been my grandfather, she told me that he had been a trainer of horses. 'Dead, now, this long while,' she had added, in her soft, sad voice.

I begged her to tell me more, but she only shook her head.

When I grew old enough to have romantic

notions, I imagined that Mother must once have cared for someone in Ireland. I suppose it was the small, redwood box which she kept hidden in a dresser drawer that had given rise to such thoughts. She had let me see into it, once, as a child. It had contained her grandmother's rosary, brought with her to America for protection, and a browned cluster of Irish flowers, with a bit of the old sod still clinging to their shriveled roots. There was a string of amber beads, as well, and a pair of dangling earrings, which Mother had told me were set with real garnets.

A book, with a leather binding, had been pressed into the bottom of the small chest, tied up with a bit of faded, pink ribbon. Mother had opened it for me. It was handwritten in some strange language—Gaelic, Mother said—and the flyleaf had been decorated with colorful illuminations. I remembered that the writing and the colors had been smeared a little, as though Mother had once wept over the stiff pages.

Then Father and Mother had died in that strange, almost planned automobile accident. I inherited the rosewood chest, with its sparce contents, and wept over Mother's few belongings.

I was brought out of the past by the pressure of Bren's arms around me.

'You must miss them both very much,' he said.

'I do,' I said. 'They were all I had. There are so many things I would like to have known about them both. Now they're gone, and I never shall. All I have left of them are a few small belongings.'

'God give them both peace,' Bren said, softly.

Later, I realized that it was this undeniably gentle side to his character that drew me so quickly to him—this cleverly concealed capacity for understanding that thrived in him, contrasting excitingly with his dark side. But perhaps it was, after all, that indescribable streak of wickedness that I had glimpsed in him which fascinated me most. I have never been quite certain. I only know that from the instant that I first saw him, I felt committed to share his life.

Now I said, 'I like to think that Mother's spirit has flown back to the homeland.'

'The wild geese always return,' Bren said. 'Sooner or later, they come back to us.'

'We were poor,' I said. 'Mother couldn't have afforded to return.'

'Then you must return in her stead,' Bren told me. 'Why not fly back with me to Ireland, Roisin? We could leave tonight, and no one the wiser.'

Speechless, I stared at him, trying desperately to see his face. Was he only teasing? Or did he mean what he said? There was no clue on his handsome features.

26

I said in a stiff, frightened voice: 'Let me go, please.'

He released me so suddenly that had it not been for his arm shooting out to steady me, I should have tumbled backward into the bay.

'I've shocked you,' he said, sounding pleased.

'Yes,' I said. 'Yes, you have.'

I turned quickly, and stifling an urge to run from him, I strode bravely off.

'Deirdre the virgin!' His voice followed me, tinged with mirth.

I was certain, as I pushed open the Yacht Club door, that I heard him laugh.

CHAPTER THREE

Catherine came to my room the next morning to gossip about the dance.

'Where did you get off to, last night, with our handsome Irish count?' she demanded, fixing me unmercifully with her dark eyes.

'We merely walked out onto the dock for a breath of air,' I said, toying with a crystal-stoppered bottle.

I felt my cheeks flush, partly because I found myself resenting Catherine's intrusion, partly because it seemed that I had behaved very foolishly there on the dock.

I guessed that Catherine was watching me,

and when I turned at last to face her, the knowing smile that I had expected was there on her face.

'You sounded absolutely defensive just then, Deirdre,' she accused. 'As though you might have allowed him to make some scandalous advance. Oh, I saw the way he looked at you, standing there in the receiving line. I had the feeling that he intended to lure you off.'

'I shall probably never see him again,' I stated.

The thought depressed me, and I changed the subject, asking Catherine about the Condesa.

'She's quite lovely,' I said, aware that I was luring Catherine on, not because the Condesa herself interested me, but because her daughter had gone to Bren's island.

'Of course,' Catherine said, with a pleased laugh. 'She comes from one of the oldest and best families in Spain. Her maiden name was De Medina. Surely, you've heard of them.'

I shook my head.

'I keep forgetting that you've not had the *advantages* that I have,' Catherine said, her laugh mocking this time, poking fun at Aunt Ruth and me both, I suspected.

It was impossible to feel angry with her. She was like a naughty child, turning herself off and on.

'A branch of the De Medina family came to California in the days of the dons,' Catherine continued. 'So you see, Angelina is actually as much a Californian as I am. She and Mother—my real mother—attended the same finishing school. And they were both married all in the same year. Mother settled for her Irishman—and Angelina captured herself a dashing polo player from the Argentine, who had come to play at Del Monte. He had loads of money, and Angelina was able to refurbish the old De Medina castle in Spain, which she had inherited a short time earlier from some shriveled old aunt. Catherine's eyes filled with fondness for her godmother. 'She took me there the year Mother died, and I've gone with her many times since.'

'I've never seen a real castle,' I said, remembering that Bren lived in one.

'You haven't missed out on a great deal,' Catherine said. 'Angelina's castle is rather dour, one of those great, Spanish-Moorish affairs, replete with a dungeon and leftovers from the Inquisition,' Catherine shuddered. 'Imagine anyone wanting to have that sort of thing lying about—torture instruments, and chests and chests of musty old parchments. Angelina sold the lot of it to some weird Irishman to put into his own castle.'

My heart started to pound with some half-formed premonition.

'Good heavens!' Catherine exclaimed, when I asked her the Irishman's name. 'There is more than one of them, you know. I assure you

29

that it was not your precious O'Leary who purchased those monstrosities, though I don't doubt that they would have complemented his personality. This particular Irishman had one of those typical Irish names that they poke fun at on the stage. Paddy something or other, Angelina called him.'

'Short for Patrick,' I said.

'Something like that. The important thing though was that the man had money. Loads of lovely money, which Angelina needed at the time. It seems that her polo-playing husband had handled his finances unwisely. He died, leaving Angelina practically penniless. Now she no longer has to concern herself with such trivia. She has lived very well since she disposed of those ugly old racks and wheels.'

'She has only herself to think of, then?'

'Herself and me,' Catherine told me, without guile. 'She is like a mother to me, since my real mother died. And since she lost Katsy.'

'How did Katsy die?' I asked. My heart pounded with a sudden sense of dread as I remembered the Condesa's suspicions.

'I don't really know,' Catherine said. 'One day Angelina simply quit talking about her, and I never saw Katsy again. It happened shortly after Angelina sold those ugly old things from the family castle. The two of them had quarreled over it. Katsy had such a passion for those old antiques. She would

30

rather have seen them starve than to part with a single garrote.'

Catherine shuddered. 'I often wondered whom she intended to dismember. I remember that one torture instrument was a bronze bull of some sort—a hideous thing, large enough to put a man inside of. Katsy told me once that the bull was used to roast people alive back in those barbarous days.'

I said, 'It seems the vogue, now, to take pleasure in such things, anything antique.'

'Katsy was furious with Angelina for selling them, that much I know. She went raging off to Ireland, determined to have her precious relics back.' Catherine shrugged. 'Some of Katsy's ideas were quite insane, really.'

I thought: And somehow, Katsy de Gomez ended up on Count Brendan O'Leary's small island.

I asked: 'Did she return from Ireland with her prize? Did she get her relics back?'

'I never saw her again,' Catherine stated. 'When I asked Angelina about her, Angelina said in this odd, dull voice: "Katsy is dead." Just that stark reply. I've always suspected that Katsy somehow got involved with a man there. It had happened before, you know. She was that sort of girl. Ravishing, and rather indiscreet. There was one rather terrible scandal one summer, while we were all there in Spain.'

I tried to picture the girl Catherine

described. If Katsy de Gomez had become amorously involved there in Ireland, had it been with Bren?

I said: 'The Condesa knows Count O'Leary.'

'Certainly,' Catherine said. 'It's a very small world, really, when one happens to have money.' She flashed me a sympathetic look. 'You've a great deal to learn about our way of life, Deirdre, I can't imagine anyone being so naive, but I really feel that I must warn you. Men like Count O'Leary aren't always to be trusted.'

I said, a little tartly, that I felt quite competent to look after myself, and in any case, it hardly seemed likely that I would ever see the man again.

A sense of loss swept through me as I said it, seeming to confirm my cousin's opinion of me.

CHAPTER FOUR

There wasn't a good deal for me to do in Uncle Con's house, where there were servants to take care of everything. I spent a lot of time imagining effortless conversations between myself and Count O'Leary in which I was carried out of the plain, fox-colored shell which was Deirdre Rynne to become some sophisticated creature of unimaginable beauty.

There had been no word from him.

I searched industriously for odd jobs to occupy myself. Nothing seemed to help. Bren was forever popping into my thoughts.

I didn't realize that I was moping about until one morning Aunt Ruth called it to my attention.

'You're looking pale lately, darling,' she said. 'You've not been getting out enough. I had hoped you would meet some nice young man, at the ball . . .' Her voice dwindled off.

I said, trying to make light of Aunt Ruth's concern: 'It's only a touch of spring fever. It happens to me every year.'

'It's quite lovely in the park these days,' Aunt Ruth said. 'You should plan an outing. The fresh air would do you good.'

It occurred to me that I hadn't been to the Japanese Tea Garden since the night of the ball. The cherry trees would be starting to bloom.

Later, looking back, I told myself that it had been fate which took me to the park that day, filling yet another blank in the puzzle that, when the pieces were all in place, would complete my destiny.

*   *   *

Bren was there, seated on a bench beneath a flowering cherry tree. It seemed somehow symbolic that I should see him this second time, with flowers fluting about his head as they had been when I first saw him the night of the ball. I felt suddenly very light-hearted and gay, thinking rather unreasonably that our meeting had been planned by some omnipotent power outside the two of us.

The truth is, I had fallen in love. I went to him, smiling.

He rose, and bent to kiss me, his lips brushing mine like the velvet wings of a butterfly.

'I thought you would never come,' he said.

'Have you come every day?' I asked.

'Every day,' he said, taking my hand.

I thought how romantic it seemed, and I tried to recall the scintillating conversations I had imagined with him. But my clever dialogue seemed to have fled. I said: 'What do you think of the Tea Garden?'

'I've not noticed it, really,' he said. 'I've been far too busy looking into faces in search of freckles.'

'How did you know I would come?' I asked.

'Because of the fairies beneath the rocks,' he said.

A sense of unreality came over me. The sun seemed incredibly bright. I felt an overwhelming urge to blurt out to Bren that I had fallen in love.

I said, instead: 'You could have called for me at the house.'

34

'I preferred to tempt fate,' he said.

We began to stroll, then, and after a while I asked him how much longer he planned to be in San Francisco.

'Only until I have convinced you that you are a wild goose destined to fly back with me to Ireland,' he said, grasping my hand.

Beneath the bright, teasing look in his eyes, I glimpsed something darkly serious. It made me uneasy, and I began to chatter on aimlessly.

I felt his eyes on me, compelling me to look at him. When I did, I caught an almost quizzical look on his face.

'Eevelleen,' he said, then, softly.

I stared at him, stunned. 'Who is Eevelleen?' I asked.

'Don't you know?' he asked. His eyes were burning into mine.

'An old flame of yours,' I said, forcing my voice to be light.

'It's an Irish endearment peculiar to we O'Learys,' he said then. 'It means little queen. It came to me how appropriate to you it is as I looked at you standing there with the sun gilding every freckle on your face.'

'If it is an endearment peculiar only to your family, how could you possibly have expected me to know what it means?' I said.

I thought: He hasn't told me the truth. He is not a man to be trusted, just as Catherine said.

I said then, in a voice trembling with some

half-formed hurt: 'And does it suit me as well as it did her?'

His brows shot up in surprise. He gripped my shoulders and spun me to face him, peering intently into my eyes. 'Aye, Eevelleen, it does, take it from me who knows,' he said, slipping easily into brogue. With his finger, he traced the contours of my nose and lips and brows.

I wanted to ask again about the girl he had once called Eevelleen. I wondered if it could possibly have been Katsy de Gomez. But he started telling me about his home, Inish Laoghaire.

'And Inish Laoghaire is a part of Ireland?' I asked instead.

'It lies off the coast of Kerry,' he told me. 'We've a mile of wild blue sea between us and the mainland, which has kept the tourists from hounding us. We've not been contaminated as they have in the rest of Ireland.'

'Which means, I suppose, that you consider yourselves more purely Irish than the rest of them,' I said.

'We O'Learys have always been proud of our native heritage,' he said.

'We?'

'My father and I,' he told me. 'There are no other true O'Learys left.'

He said this last with a hint of sadness, and I wondered if perhaps some members of his family had met with tragedy.

'The two of you live alone there, then?'

'There are others,' he said abruptly, and his face grew grim.

'You live in a castle there on your island,' I stated.

He glanced sharply at me. 'How did you know that?' he demanded. 'Who has been talking to you about me?' He seemed almost savage.

'My cousin Catherine told me,' I said quickly. 'She heard it from Uncle Con, who, of course, is Irish and knows about the places there. Does it really matter so much?' I added, with a nervous laugh.

He became suddenly docile.

'It's just that I had hoped to fill you in on the details of my life myself,' he said. 'Others have a peculiar habit of distorting the facts.' He smiled at me quite pleasantly. 'Dunleary. That's the name of my castle. We've made our home there for over three hundred years.'

'It's difficult for me to imagine anyone living that long in the same house.' I gave him an amazed smile. 'Our family record was three years. That was the cottage in Ohio, near the faery mounds.'

An ache came into my throat, and I wished suddenly that I had been born into a stable, old castle. It sounded like a secure place.

And then I remembered that Catherine had mentioned a legend.

'There must be any number of ghosts

hovering about your castle by now,' I said.

'We've no ghosts at Dunleary,' he stated.

I thought I detected an edge of displeasure to his voice. I didn't quite dare to ask him outright about the legend.

We had come to the gate at the entrance to the Tea Garden. My bus was there. Aunt Ruth expected me home by six. She would worry, I told Bren, if I didn't arrive on schedule. I asked Bren then if he would come to dinner. Uncle Con and Aunt Ruth had told me that I should feel free to ask my friends in. There hadn't been anyone until now.

'We're located on the rich side of Russian Hill, as Catherine defines it,' I said, giving him the name of the street, 'I'm certain you can find it. A large, stucco house . . .'

His eyes clouded.

'I would like to, Deirdre, very much,' he said. 'But I've a previous engagement. If I might beg off . . .'

'Certainly,' I said, not quite believing him.

His voice had sounded slightly stilted, its charm neutralized by a hint of coldness. I guessed that he dreaded an encounter with Catherine, probably because of her resemblance to Katsy de Gomez. Or had I repulsed him some way by seeming too eager?

He flashed me a smile as the bus pulled off, looking rather innocent standing there against the backdrop of cherry blossoms.

CHAPTER FIVE

I saw a good deal of Bren after that. He had rented a car, and he called for me often.

I found that I was coming to count on his presence, and this disturbed me a little, for I couldn't yet be certain what he wanted of me. Several times I looked up, when we were together, to find him watching me, as though comparing me with some other girl.

I felt unsettled, mercurial, my emotions running the gamut between soaring ecstasy and utter despair. I lived in constant dread of losing him. And although I was not fully aware of it at the time, my apprehension gave our relationship savor. I felt obsessed to enjoy every minute I spent with him to its fullest.

I shall never forget the first time he kissed me, not as he had kissed me there at the ball, or in the Tea Garden, but with passion.

We were in Golden Gate Park that day, strolling along the bridle trails. A slight breeze rattled the eucalyptus leaves above our heads. Here and there, small bands of sheep grazed the lush meadows, and Bren remarked that they reminded him of Ireland.

'It makes me eager to be back,' he said, his eyes filled with yearning. 'I've been away far too long.'

I had dreaded this moment, and had tried to

prepare myself for it.

'I've enjoyed our outings,' I said, in a voice that sounded strained, even to my own ears. 'Though I imagine that I shall learn to live without them.'

He came close to me, pushing his face very near to my own.

'You absurd child,' he said, and I was swept into an embrace that snatched my breath away. 'Why do you think I have stayed on here like this?' he demanded.

'To attend to whatever business that brought you here, and to see the city,' I said, in a weak voice.

'Haven't you heard anything I have said to you these past days?' he asked. 'In God's name, Deirdre! I've had every intention of taking you back to Ireland with me from the first moment we met!'

'But I thought you were only teasing,' I said.

His eyes darkened. He kissed me then, hungrily. Savagely. When he released me, my mouth ached. My heart thudded monstrously.

'Do you think now that I am only teasing?' he demanded. A muscle worked along the hard line of his jaw. Above it, his eyes were brooding.

I gave him a tentative smile. Then I recalled his words to the Condesa. Pulling away from him, I walked primly a few steps down the path.

'I can't just go off with you,' I said, over my

40

shoulder. 'Surely you understand that.'

'Deirdre the virgin!' he said, as he had that night on the pier. There was the same note of mirth lilting suddenly in his voice, and something else. Approval! I thought, amazed.

I swung to face him. Miraculously, his anger had fled. 'Sure, Roisin,' he said, slipping into brogue. 'It is you I intend to make my wife.'

I felt slightly dizzy, and drew a deep breath to clear my head. 'Why have you chosen me?' I asked in a remarkably calm voice.

He shook his head in puzzled amusement.

'Sure, some women will come to you on a spider's thread with no thought for the consequences, while others, the brace of a ship won't pull without the proper speeches.' He paused, coming to grip me by the shoulders, his fingers biting into my flesh. 'Isn't it enough, mavourneen, that I've set my heart on having you?' His eyes glowed wickedly beneath his satanic brows. 'Deirdre the virgin!' he whispered, leaning to kiss me again.

'Why do you insist on calling me that?' I asked, feeling irritated with him.

'You've not read the *Tain bo Cualnge*—the famous Cattle Raid of Cooley?' he asked.

I shook my head.

'You shall,' he said confidently. 'And when you do, you shall see that Deirdre was educated for the pleasure of a king. And as such, she was, of course, a virgin.'

He seemed terribly pompous and arrogant.

41

'But you are only a count,' I retorted.

'I am The O'Leary,' he said. 'Descendent of Leary, King of Tara. He was an extremely important personage in Ireland. On my island they call me king.'

'And if it should happen that I weren't a virgin?' I said daringly, his exalted manner making me rebellious.

'If I were to discover that you are a wanton, I should strangle you with my bare hands and toss your body to the basking sharks off Inish Laoghaire,' he said in a low, fierce voice.

I thought at once of Katsy de Gomez. Had she been a wanton? Catherine had said as much. Was that the reason she had died? And, if so, who had killed her? Bren?

No! I pushed the frightening thoughts from my mind.

Perhaps I might have agreed to marry him that day if it had not been for that undercurrent of thoughts.

'I've no intention of marrying anyone, just yet,' I said rather primly.

'We shall see,' Bren said, undaunted.

I knew that it was only a matter of time before I would relent.

CHAPTER SIX

It occurred to me that Catherine was taking quite an interest in my relationship with Bren. Often, she appeared on the stairs when he called for me, smiling down at us as we left the house, her face lighted with a provocative smile. There were other times when she flirted openly with him. But Bren yielded nothing of himself to her, and this, I am certain, continued to amaze her, for she was accustomed to a good deal of attention from men.

We were alone in my room one day, and I told my cousin that Bren had asked me to marry him.

She looked at me, stunned.

'If you tell me that you have accepted his proposal, I shall never forgive you.' She gave a vicious little laugh.

'But for goodness sake, why?'

'Because I am disappointed in Count O'Leary,' she said. 'He is utterly unromantic, and even though you have sandy hair, and freckles, you deserve a good deal more than some barbarous Irishman who goes about in a black mood.' She flashed me a redeeming smile. 'You really could be quite attractive, though.'

I said to Catherine: 'You have never

forgiven him, have you, for not kissing your cheek there at the ball?'

'Would you?' she demanded. 'It was terribly rude of him, you know, to ignore me like that. I suppose I am a spiteful bitch. But I would like very much to get even.'

'Has it ever occurred to you that perhaps he can't help being the way he is?' I said, thinking of Katsy de Gomez. 'It's quite possible that some stunning, dark-haired creature took advantage of him once, so that he can no longer trust any of you.'

'So he has asked you to marry him,' Catherine remarked, not really pacified by my compliment. 'Because you are plain and shan't ever betray him.' She rushed to fling her arms about me in an unexpected and rather false gesture of affection. 'I don't mean that cruelly, darling. But you are really rather insignificant, you know, when it comes to looks. And some men feel absolutely safe in marrying a plain girl. Essentially, they are cowards.'

'Whatever his reasons,' I said, suddenly weary of her, 'I haven't yet made up my mind.'

Glancing at my watch, I drew away from her. Bren was to call for me at one.

'Or perhaps it is a *mariage de convenance* he has in mind?' Catherine rushed on. 'You know that they still believe in that sort of thing there in Ireland. They are a practical lot, I understand. He does lots of business with Father, you know.'

44

'You are much more angry with him than I had imagined,' I said, stunned by Catherine's words.

'I dislike being snubbed by handsome men,' Catherine pouted. For once, she didn't laugh.

'It's not true, you know, what you are thinking,' I said. 'If he had wanted a business advantage with Uncle Con, he'd have chosen you. As it is, his entire reason for being here in America is to claim me!' I blurted it out before I quite realized what I was saying.

It was Catherine's turn to stare, her brown eyes round with surprise. 'For God's sake, Deirdre, you never saw the man before in your life. How could he possibly have known you existed? Or have you been keeping secrets from us. Perhaps he's someone out of your mother's past. Is that it, Deirdre? He is a good deal older than we are, you know.' She stared at me with suspicious eyes. 'Father always suspected your mother of having some black secret behind her.'

'Bren is only twenty-seven,' I said, feeling suddenly deflated. 'He would have been only a child when Mother left Ireland. And even if he were out of Mother's past, what on earth could he possibly want with me?'

Tears of doubt and frustration welled in my eyes. What *did* Bren want with me? Had he been so disillusioned by beauty that he must, as my cousin suggested, seek out someone mousy?

I wanted him to marry me for far better reasons.

CHAPTER SEVEN

The currents of air sweeping up over the Point Lobos Cliffs were misty and heavy with salt. An expression of pleasure came onto Bren's face, as we stepped from the rented car to enter Cliff House.

'It smells like the homeland,' he said, his eyes gleaming with delight. 'Why have we waited so long to come here?'

'Because there has been so much else to see,' I said, thinking how remarkably well the olive green of his sweater suited his browned complexion. 'The Post Office murals,' I continued, listing the places we had been together. 'Coit Tower. The wax museum.' I paused, looking into his face.

His eyes darkened briefly. There had been something about the wax museum that had displeased him; I had sensed it in him the day we went there.

'None of it can compare to the sight and sound of the open sea,' Bren said now.

Inside, seated at one of the tables, which were arranged before the sweep of blue-tinted windows, Bren's eyes kept straying to the sea, which was there almost directly below us.

'Have you ever seen anything so savage?' I said.

'Aye,' he said, going into brogue.

'Where?' I demanded.

'Inish Laoghaire,' he stated. 'We've powerful seas there. They beat at us unmercifully from end to end of year. We've seas there that no man could hope to conquer.'

'Is it always that way? Are there never any days when the seas grow docile?'

'A few perhaps,' he told me. 'At times, we've cornflower waters around us, clear, when you gaze down into them from a curragh. But very deceptive. You can see great schools of mackerel there, and the sharks, dark as sin, skimming by. But it is more often savage than tame.'

'What is a curragh?' I asked, fascinated by this wild, far-off place he described.

'The boats we use there, to commute with the mainland. They are made of lathes, covered with tarred canvas, and ride the waves like eggshells.'

He was unable to keep his eyes from the sea as he spoke, and I fancied, as I sat watching the small movements of his tanned face, that it brought out the untamed in him. That he was perhaps as savage as the wild seas he described.

'And you are king of all of that wild sea,' I said.

'As O'Learys have been from the days of

47

King Leary at Tara,' he said. 'Just as our sons shall be. A son for each mile of land on Inish Laoghaire, and each of them bearing the proud crest of Leary!' He flashed his large ring at me.

My heart pounded at his daring inference, and I tried desperately to think of some tart reply that would let him know that I was not to be an easy conquest.

The waitress came then with our orders of fried shrimp, and when she had gone, the proper moment to rebuke him had vanished.

I said, instead: 'I still don't understand about your being a count.'

'The title is French,' he explained. 'A courtesy paid to one of my ancestors when he took refuge in that country, during the time of the Irish penal laws. I suppose we've clung to it out of some false sense of vanity.' His voice became suddenly bitter.

'But you've said yourself that you are king on Inish Laoghaire,' I reminded him.

'The Aran Islands, the Blaskets have their kings as well. It's a custom on the offshore islands. No more than that. Although I intend to give it some greater significance on Inish Laoghaire. I shall make something of that barren piece of stone, I assure you.'

'You seem to have done well there so far,' I said, remembering what Catherine had told me about his scattered wealth.

'It's not there that I've prospered,' he said.

'Although I have always gone back to the homeland with my earnings, picking up where those before me left off. I've the means now to carry on what was begun there in Ireland, centuries ago, by my ancestors. I'll realize their dreams for them.

'Now that I've found you, Roisin, I can do anything,' he added very softly, his voice making my heart leap.

Then suddenly I felt uneasy, for I imagined that I detected something else in his bright eyes—a certain remoteness, as though he weren't seeing me at all, but that other girl. *Eevelleen*, whoever she might have been.

*   *   *

When we finished with our lunch, I asked him if he wanted to see Mile Rock, since we were already in the vicinity. I imagined that it must be something like his island, and I thought that it might please him for that reason.

'There are six men stranded there day and night,' I said. 'Although it is only a half mile from the shore. But it might as well be in China, with the wild seas crashing about it. At times, they say, it is dashed completely under.'

Perhaps because I knew that I could not keep him in San Francisco much longer, that he was eager to get back to Ireland, and that he was not a man to be delayed by the whims of a woman, I rattled on about the sights, trying to make them sound as interesting as possible.

'I'll see your rock,' he said. 'Though I doubt if it can compare to mine,' he added, giving me a mischievous look.

We left Cliff House, and he drew me suddenly into an opening between the gray buildings and kissed me.

A young couple walked by on the steps, and when Bren finally released me, I guessed by the amused expressions on their faces that they had been watching us. I pulled away from Bren, my face burning.

The girl, who was very fashionable in trim shorts and a ribbed sweater, gave a little laugh at my confusion. She twined her arm around her young man, and kissed his cheek, and the two of them went on down the steps, the girl giving Bren an arch look over her shoulder, conveying to him that all girls were not the prude I seemed to be.

'You are a bog cotton tassel,' Bren said when they had gone, and I fancied that he seemed pleased that they had caught us.

'I've no idea what you're talking about,' I retorted, feeling slightly irritated and a little foolish.

'A bog cotton tassel is a charming little Irish flower. It is a virginal flower, delicate and pure. I much prefer it over the bolder blooms. Fuchsias, for instance. Fuchsias, at least in Ireland, are very profuse, thrusting their bright blossoms blatantly about, climbing shamelessly over everything.'

Suddenly, some of the joy vanished from his face. His soaring brows beetled. I fancied that he seemed almost bitter. Then the mood passed, and he was himself once more, excited by the nearness of the sea, catching me to him again.

I protested, saying that someone else would surely come along and catch us there in the little alley.

'It's time I made love to you,' he said, smiling at my apprehension. 'I shall captivate you so thoroughly that you shall have no other choice than to go home with me to Dunleary.'

He kissed me again, fiercely, his mouth demanding.

CHAPTER EIGHT

The view of Mile Rock was superb that day. I stood beside Bren, feeling the breeze on my lips, which still burned from his kiss. He had made it quite clear to me there on the steps beside Cliff House—he was ready now to claim me.

But why me? I wondered, time and again. How had he even known that I existed? I recalled the way he had first looked at me from beneath the bower of flowers decorating

51

the lounge doorway. There had been a gleam of triumph in his eyes, as though he had ended a quest.

It occurred to me that there had been a certain strategy behind his wooing of me, and I felt uneasy. I thought: I should get away now, while I am still free. Then I looked up into his darkly handsome face, and I realized that I wasn't free at all, that already I had waited too long.

I told Bren, as we stood gazing out at the upthrusting, black rock, that fragments of ships were said still to be visible, caught up on the rocks. No doubt there were rare treasures there, I said, for all of this had once belonged to the Spanish, who loved gold, and had transported Aztec treasures from Mexico in their galleons.

At my mention of the Spanish, I felt him go suddenly stiff. His face became grim, and he grasped my arm savagely, wheeling me about, turning his back on the sea which I knew he loved. He walked with long, vicious steps to where the car stood near the railing, and I found myself trailing helplessly in his wake.

He headed the car south, toward Daly City, Edgemar and Pacific Manor, leaving the San Francisco Memorial, with its view of Mile Rock, behind. I sat very still beside him, aware of his vigorous body so close beside my own.

He gripped the wheel with determined hands, and I sensed in him a newly pressing

52

urgency, which I found rather frightening. I realized how uncertain of him I was.

We were on Highway 1, which clings precariously above the Pacific; the ocean shone a deceptive blue and was scattered over with a few dark shadows of clouds. Gradually, as we plummeted southward, Bren relented a little, his dark mood lifting by degrees.

After a while, he said: 'This seems the sort of drive where lovers might find some appropriate niche to themselves.' He flashed me a relentless smile. 'I've an overwhelming urge to kiss you again. It's time we settled things between us, and I can think of no more appropriate place than here, within sight and sound of the rolling sea. It inspires me,' he added, a hint of that former savagery in his voice.

His bright eyes promised a good deal more than an innocent kiss, and I folded my hands primly in my lap. I wondered wildly what I should do if he took me to some secluded spot and tried to make love to me.

He sensed my withdrawal. 'You're afraid of me,' he stated, and I imagined that he sounded pleased, as though my fear somehow enhanced his conquest.

'Kissing is really quite new to me,' I said.

'Bog cotton tassel,' he accused, in a soft voice. He was delighted by my prudishness. 'An infant still, and unspoiled. I shall mold you to suit my every whim!'

53

'It shan't be as easy as you seem to imagine,' I retorted. 'I've been permitted to run wild.'

He became very intense. 'If you are preparing to tell me that you are not the innocent that I have believed, I shall strangle you now and have done with it,' he threatened. 'Deirdre the virgin,' he added in a muted voice.

'I only meant that I received little discipline with Mother ill, and Father drinking. I was let go,' I said, suddenly repulsed by a thought of those strong, slim hands folding about my throat. He would do it, I thought, without a qualm. 'I used to slip off to the woods to sit on a fairy mound, imagining all sorts of fantastic things,' I added.

'You were always alone in your wood, those times?'

'Except when Mother was well enough to walk with me and Father was sober,' I said. 'I had a girl friend, too, for a while. A long-legged child named Becky. She deserted me, however. Mother's nose began to bleed once, while Becky was there. I had to pack it.' I glanced at Bren. 'Hemorrhages happen in all forms of leukemia, and I had learned what I must do for Mother. It frightened Becky terribly to see Mother's blood flowing. I suppose it would have frightened any girl. And of course, there was Father's drinking—he must have seemed very strange to her, too. Anyhow, Becky avoided me after that, as though I were the one with some baffling disease.'

'People are like that,' Bren said. 'About someone different,' he added. 'And you were, you know. You still are. You are the sort of girl who shan't be frightened by the old Count.'

'The old Count?' I asked, giving him a startled look.

'My father,' he said.

'Is he ill?'

'In quite a different way from your mother,' he said. 'With father, it is a condition of the mind.' I must have looked frightened, for he added quickly, 'He's quite harmless, really. It's only that his mind wanders at times. Other times, he is quite rational, though he forgets things. He paints a little, and writes a good deal of poetry.'

'How long has he been this way?' I asked, thinking of the little book tucked into the bottom of Mother's rosewood chest. Did the old Count write his poetry in Gaelic, I wondered, suddenly curious.

'For twenty years,' Bren said, a hint of mystery coming into his voice, giving the number some hidden significance. 'In all of that time, he hasn't left the island, except to be rowed about the sea on a fair day.'

'That's a long while to be shut away from the world,' I said. 'I suppose he has his reasons.'

'He does, though there are those who

55

'wouldn't understand,' Bren said.

'And you do?' I asked.

'There was a girl once,' Bren said. 'We were both in love with her.'

'You must have been only a child,' I said.

'I was old enough at the time to fall in love, as small boys sometimes do, with an older woman,' Bren said.

'I've heard of little boys falling in love with their schoolteacher,' I said. 'Was that what she was?'

'There was a good deal more to it than that,' Bren stated grimly.

His mouth set in a firm line, and I knew that he had told me all that he intended. It occurred to me that if I should marry Bren, I would be going off to some weird, old castle peopled with strangers.

I fancied that the very walls of Dunleary would be permeated with all sorts of strange memories. Was the secret of Katsy de Gomez's death locked away there? Were the O'Learys murderers, as the Condesa suspected? What had happened to the woman both Bren and his father had loved? Had they murdered her, too?

Dunleary seemed very far away, and rather unreal, like the fairy castle in a nursery rhyme. And because I visualized myself romantically, as a heroine of some sort whose eventual presence, should I decide to marry Bren, would somehow banish all darkness and evil

56

deeds, it was difficult for me then to take the dark questions as seriously as I should have.

Later that day, Bren asked me again to marry him, and, carried away by my romantic vision of him, I accepted. We were married very quietly the following week and left for Ireland on the same day.

CHAPTER NINE

On the plane, I asked Bren about his family.

'You said there were others at Dunleary besides you and your father,' I reminded him. 'I want to know all about them. Everything.'

'Not quite, darling,' he said. 'There are some things about my family not fit for the ears of a virgin bride. We've not been perfect there at Dunleary.'

Beneath his smile, I glimpsed something that seemed almost to be a warning. I remembered that Catherine had mentioned a legend, the night of the ball, so scandalous that Uncle Con had refused to reveal it to her, and I guessed that it was behind Bren's reluctance to have me know all about his family.

'You've some weird ghost tale connected with the castle,' I accused in a persistent voice. 'And you're afraid that it might frighten me. Mother told me once that everything in Ireland has a story behind it. Even the fairy mounds.'

He turned toward me rather fiercely.

'You'll not be believing every wild tale you hear in Ireland,' he commanded.

I stifled an urge to shrink from his fiery gaze, remembering that, although our vows hadn't yet been consummated, he was now my husband.

'I've always been quite sensible,' I said, with forced calm. 'For all of Mother's distracting fairy stories. I believe that I shall be capable of sorting the fact from the fiction.'

'Sure even we who live there have trouble doing that,' he said, slipping into brogue.

I was certain then that there was something that he wanted to keep from me, for I had found that to be a habit of his when he was deeply disturbed.

I looked at the proud, Gaelic lines of his face, so close beside my own, and it occurred to me suddenly that I was going off alone with a stranger. The feeling exhilarated me, for the doubts hadn't yet begun in earnest.

After a brief silence, Bren began rather grudgingly, to tell me about his family. There was no enthusiasm in his voice as he spoke, and I fancied that he seemed displeased with them.

'You already know about the old Count,' he said. 'I know that you shall be good for him— that his . . . affliction shan't frighten you. We humor him. He's very easily pleased.'

58

'There were many times when I found it necessary to humor my own father,' I said, my voice trembling slightly at the memory. 'I expect that I shall get on with the old Count.'

'I imagine that you could get on well with anyone, Roisin.' Bren's voice became tender, his eyes intimate. 'It seems to be a quality of the innocent that they see nothing but good in others.'

'And you have chosen me because you imagine that I shall never become aware of your wickedness,' I said, giving a little laugh of relief.

'I hope that you shall never be subjected to the details of my black past,' Bren said. He returned my smile. But there was a note of seriousness in his voice.

'I believe you mean that,' I accused.

'What would you do if you discovered that I had been terribly wicked?' he asked.

Something of my perplexity must have shown in my face, for suddenly he laughed, and became very gay. 'But of course you shan't, for I've been very careful to cover my evil tracks,' he added, leaning to kiss me and whispering mischievously into my ear.

'Deirdre the virgin,' he said. 'I'm convinced that it would be impossible for you to see anything but the best, even in me.'

'So long as you meant what you said about having lost your keenness for fuchsias,' I retorted, trying to match his light mood, which,

I thought, seemed slightly forced. 'You were telling me about your family. Remember?'

'After the old Count comes my brother, Padraic,' he said, his enthusiasm waning. I felt again that he disliked the people who lived with him in Dunleary. 'My half-brother, actually. Padraic is the son of Father's first wife. He's forty—a dozen years older than myself, which may account for the fact that we seem to have little in common.'

'Your father waited, then, before he remarried,' I said.

'He had two wives between Padraic's mother and mine,' Bren stated. 'You might say that Father has been unlucky in love.'

'But what happened?' I asked.

'They all died.' His voice became bitter.

'Natural deaths?'

'Accidental.' Bren said, not looking at me.

'Your mother, too?'

'My mother died when I was five,' he stated. 'She died bearing Father another son. Neither of them survived the ordeal. We've no doctor there on Inish Laoghaire,' he added, giving me a quick look. 'I shall bring Dr. Riordan over from the mainland when your own time comes. I'll not have you submitted to the uncertain manipulations of a midwife. Mrs. Kelly delivered mother. She's a trained nurse, though she had no power over childbed fever.'

'She's still there, then?'

'She cares for Mrs. Maguire.' His eyes had

60

grown very bright, as though, I thought, he were on the verge of divulging some thrilling secret. 'My old nanny,' he added. 'She happens to own the small island next to ours. Maguire Island, it's called.'

'But I thought that you were quite isolated there on your Inish Laoghaire,' I said.

'There is no one living now on Maguire Island. Technically, it is a part of Inish Laoghaire. There's not more than a stone's throw between the two. It has always been my theory that a portion of Inish Laoghaire became submerged, in some eon past, when the earth's crust gave way.'

'It seems that your ancestor might have claimed it for the O'Learys, then, if it is so near,' I said.

'The Maguires were there a step ahead of us, having been driven from their own lands by the English, just as we were.'

'And this Mrs. Maguire still owns it?'

'She is the last of them, although she lives with us at Dunleary. Father brought her there, after my mother died, to care for me. She has never gone back to her island.'

'What will happen to it, then?'

'Perhaps we O'Learys shall have it at last,' Bren stated.

I glanced at him, and was amazed by the look of determination in his eyes.

'You've tried to buy it from the Maguires, then,' I said.

'Aye,' he said. 'Though you can't buy an acre of land on any of the offshore islands. People there cling to their small holdings. It is all they have.'

'Adding Maguire Island to your domain means a good deal to you, doesn't it?'

'Aye, Roisin, it does. Almost as much as having you.'

I wondered again, why he had chosen me. I felt certain that there had to be a reason of some sort, although I had no idea what it might be.

'You said that Mrs. Kelly cares for Mrs. Maguire,' I said. 'Is she ill, then?'

'She has suffered a stroke. She no longer gets about.'

The thought came to me that he was waiting for Mrs. Maguire to die, so that he could claim her island. I pushed it hurriedly from my mind.

'And who else is isolated with you, there at Dunleary?' I asked, with a forced brightness.

'I shouldn't want you to think that we have no communication there,' he objected. 'We've all of the large newspapers arriving regularly by mail from London. New York . . .' he paused.

'And San Francisco,' I prompted.

'Of course,' he said lightly. I fancied that he avoided my eyes for a moment.

Then he said: 'You wanted to know about the rest of them there at Dunleary.'

'I'm most particularly interested in family,' I

62

said. 'After all, I am now an O'Leary.' I gave a little laugh, for it all seemed rather unreal.

'In addition to the old Count and Padraic, there's Maeve,' he said. 'Padraic's aunt. A sister to Father's first wife Maeve came to Dunleary when Father married her sister. That was over forty years ago. Maeve has been with us ever since. She assisted Mrs. Kelly with Mother. Served as night nurse . . .' His voice dwindled off on a questioning note, and I imagined that something about Maeve dismayed him.

'She has never married then?'

'No. She's devoted to Padraic, and to her religion, I suppose. At any rate, she had some vague notion of becoming a nun at one time. She never did. Nevertheless, she's affected a saintly costume for herself, although there is nothing official about it. Flowing white robes. Sandals on her feet. You'd never guess that Maeve is in her early fifties, to see her face. A life of *purity* seems to have agreed with her.' He emphasized the word, purity, and I fancied that I detected a note of irony in his voice.

'Your brother, Padraic,' I said, then. 'Is he also a count? You see, I know nothing about these things. I suppose that I am now a countess.'

'You are, darling. However, Padraic is simply that: Padraic.' There was a subtle change in his voice.

'But he's the eldest,' I insisted.

'Padraic was a so-called seven-month child,' Bren stated. 'Father has never been certain that Padraic is actually his son.'

He turned dark eyes on me, the pupils dilated with some new urgency, so that the bright flecks of gold were crowded out.

'Do you understand now why your absolute innocence is so important to me?' he demanded in a tense voice. 'I shan't live my life burdened as Father has been all these years, by insidious doubts.'

He clutched my wrist until it ached, as though he could force me to be pure by the very pressure of his hand.

I became aware of the passengers across the aisle casting curious glances our way.

'Please,' I whispered. 'You're making a spectacle.' I drew primly away.

'Deirdre the virgin!' he said, in a soft, approving voice.

In that moment, I fancied that I at last understood him, and the doubt that had plagued me earlier fled. I felt foolishly secure, and even a bit smug, for I knew myself well enough to be certain that I would never betray him.

It didn't occur to me that even then I was the one betrayed.

CHAPTER TEN

We landed at Shannon Airport. An overwhelming feeling of excitement came over me as the plane taxied to a stop, and I realized that I was actually in Ireland. The homeland. Unexpectedly, Mother's name for her native land came to me.

'You are an Irishwoman now,' Bren stated, grinning. 'And I shan't ever let you forget it. The first thing I must do is teach you the old language. We've a few old fishermen in the village on Inish Laoghaire who have no English in their mouths.'

A moment later I caught a pretty hostess watching Bren as he went to fetch our luggage, a definite expression of recognition warming her blue eyes. Because I was curious and perhaps a bit jealous of that warm, bright look following after him, I distracted her with a question.

'Where might I find the ladies' lounge?' I asked.

'*Mna,* it is here, for women,' she informed me. '*Fir* for men.'

To my surprise, she followed me into the ladies' room, a cozy smile on her face. It occurred to me that it was a smile which deliberately invited a confidence, and I realized that she was as curious about me as I was about her.

Her blue eyes shone. There was no denying her attractiveness in her trim uniform. Miss Monahan, her name plaque read. I wondered suddenly what she had to do with Bren.

'It's The O'Leary you're traveling with,' she said.

I nodded numbly. I found myself suddenly resenting this attractive young hostess, with her smart good looks.

'I'd not be knowing him personally,' she said quickly. 'It's his photograph that has made him familiar here. Sure he's a handsome man, and one that a girl would not soon be forgetting. Forgive me for running on like this, but it's the article that did it.'

'Article?' I said, giving her a blank look.

'A write-up published recently in *Eire Beckons*,' she explained. 'It's a magazine done up here for export, designed to tempt the tourists. It features stories on our antiquities here, and the old legends.'

'I haven't seen it,' I said.

'There is no reason why you should, coming from America as you do,' she said. 'It was a piece on Inish Laoghaire that I saw, and the old castle there. Dunleary. The story was illustrated with photographs of the castle and The O'Leary astride his handsome horses. You'd know all about his steeplechasers, I'd assume, since it would not be like a man to keep quiet about his hobby.' The curiosity was

66

back in her eyes.

'The O'Leary isn't like other men,' I said, a bit shortly.

Bren had never mentioned horses to me. I thought, dismayed: This hostess, who is a stranger to Bren, knows more about him than I do, and I am his wife.

'I hope the photos did him justice,' I continued, striving to keep an edge of bitterness from my voice.

'They were quite good, really, with the Forest of Cratloe showing in the background. They were snapped at the demesne of the Duchess of Chelmsford, who has a stable near there, though she's no horse to equal Arkle, who has won the Cheltenham Gold Cup these three years past.'

'I know nothing about horses,' I said, a bit impatiently.

I was reminded suddenly of Mother's father, who had been a horse trainer here in the homeland. I recalled mentioning that fact to Bren. Even then, Bren had failed to reveal to me his own interest in horses. Why? It seemed to be the sort of thing a man would be eager to tell, especially to the one with whom he chose to share his life.

'Are you a secretary?' the stewardess asked candidly.

'No. No I'm not,' I said. 'I'm the Countess O'Leary.' I tried to sound regal and failed. 'I . . . I've only just married him,' I confessed then, in a small voice.

The girl flashed me a look of amazement.

'God between you and harm!' she exclaimed. 'It's not every young woman who would be willing to settle for life on that remote island. They say that The O'Leary seldom leaves it. He has an agent in Dublin, according to the article, who travels about attending to his affairs.'

But he himself came to San Francisco, I wanted to say, to attend to his affairs with Uncle Con.

I remembered what I had overheard him tell the Condesa de Gomez in the Yacht Club library: 'I intend to claim Deirdre Rynne.' Had that been his reason for coming to San Francisco, after all? Had his business with Uncle Con been irrelevant?

'You've seen Inish Laoghaire? Dunleary?' I asked the stewardess.

'As much of it as can be glimpsed from the mainland,' she said. 'I passed by last fall, on a commercial tour. The mist lifted for a moment, and we were allowed a glimpse of the old castle. A wild place, it seemed, full of vigorous Irishmen, they say, and the elderly. According to the article, there is only a handful of women, and all of them well past their prime. The O'Leary is king over all of it,' she added. 'The title belongs to the strongest among them; the most clever with a curragh. And of course The O'Leary has his wealth in his favor; everyone knows he is a rich man, and owner of the island. There is a certain romance to it all, I suppose. I can understand your desire to go there, in spite of the black legend.'

She glanced quickly at her watch and flashed me an apologetic smile. 'Forgive me for running on. And no excuse for it either. We're keen for a good story here, and the article captured my interest, with the photos of the count, and him looking so handsome. I couldn't resist having a word with you, since I hadn't the courage to approach The O'Leary.'

She hurried off then, before I could ask about the legend.

CHAPTER ELEVEN

We spent the next few weeks of what was to be our honeymoon roving over Ireland. I shall never forget how happy Bren made me during that time. He was a clever and demanding lover, more passionate than I had imagined in my most daring dreams. I wished that this happy time might never end and when Bren told me we were leaving for Kilmara, I was strangely apprehensive.

Kilmara, Bren told me, was the mainland village which commanded a view of his island. From there, he said, we would be taken by boat to Inish Laoghaire.

'I am curious about the village on Inish Laoghaire,' I said. 'And your steeplechasers,' I added, looking deliberately at him, accusing him with my eyes for not having been the one to mention them to me. I had been waiting for this moment for several weeks now.

We were headed southwest out of Shannon, along a narrow, deserted road, and it seemed to me that for the barest instant the small car wavered.

Bren flashed me a startled look. Then suddenly his face became guarded.

'All Irish villages are alike,' he said evasively. 'We've a main thoroughfare, of sorts, lined with the usual cottages, and a shop or two. There's a small grocery, which doubles as a pub. At any rate, the wine of the country, which happens to be Guinness Stout, is dispensed there. Our people don't require a good deal more. They're quite content to wear homespun and pampooties, and eat what they can catch from the sea.'

'It sounds absolutely frugal,' I stated. 'And what, for goodness sakes, are pampooties?'

He smiled suddenly. With relief, I thought, because I hadn't insisted about the horses.

'Lesson number two,' he said. 'Pampooties are foot-wear—odd little boots that we islanders sometimes wear. *Brosa ur leatair* we call them. Pampooties is a bastardization of some sort, I suspect, I'll not have you calling them that. Now say it for me, in the Irish.'

I repeated the words dutifully, and as I did so, I was overwhelmed by a sense of unreality. What was I, Deirdre Rynne, doing here in this strange place?

'I'll make you a pair,' he said, pleased, when I had mastered the odd, Gaelic words. 'And a pair for each of our sons.'

'You seem very certain that we shall have sons,' I said, resenting him just a little for his decisiveness.

'Aye. The island is an idyllic place for children. We had great times there.' There was nostalgia in his voice.

'You and Padraic?'

'Padraic?' He looked puzzled for an instant, and I guessed that it had not been his brother, Padraic, whom he had been thinking of, although he pretended at once that it had. 'We called him Paddy,' he said.

Paddy. The name seemed familiar. I remembered then that it had been the name of the Irishman who, Catherine told me, had purchased the Condesa de Gomez's family antiques.

Had Katsy de Gomez come to Inish Laoghaire, then, to retrieve the priceless bronze bull and other antiques that her mother had sold? Was Bren's brother, Padraic, the man who had purchased them? If so, I thought, Bren had had nothing to do with it. I felt suddenly buoyant with relief.

71

'That hostess at the airport recognized you from a photo she had seen in a magazine,' I said. 'She told me that nearly everyone on Inish Laoghaire is either vigorously male or elderly. Does that mean that there are no children on Inish Laoghaire?'

'Then that's how you knew about the steeplechasers,' Bren countered, giving me an accusing look.

'You make them seem almost mysterious,' I said. 'Is there any reason why I shouldn't know?'

'I'd no idea that you were interested,' Bren said evasively.

'My grandfather was a horse trainer,' I reminded him. I gave a little laugh, thinking that the moment was becoming far too serious. In another instant we would be arguing. 'Surely you haven't forgotten,' I added. 'Or does it seem important to me only because it is the single concrete item I ever managed to glean about my mother's past?'

'The photos in the magazine were taken before—' He broke off, forcing a small cough. 'Before I went to America,' he continued lamely.

For an instant I imagined that he was on the verge of confiding in me. Then, as though he had considered carefully and decided against it, he said in a grim voice: 'I thought of giving up the horses.'

'But why?' I asked. 'It seems a dashing thing

for the King of the Island to go riding about on his prancing steed. I can imagine that you must look rather like that first King Leary, who ruled his kingdom from Mount Tara.'

'I've lost interest,' he said sharply. The expression on his face warned me not to pursue the topic.

'Is it true what the hostess said about there being mostly men on your island?' I asked again, returning to a seemingly safe topic.

'I'm afraid so,' he said.

'And there are no children at all?'

Again, there was a pause, charged with some incomprehensible significance.

'There are no children,' Bren said, at last, without looking at me.

'How odd it must seem,' I commented.

I felt suddenly that he was lying to me. I glanced out of the window, trying desperately to overcome the feeling of hurt that rose in me.

He must have sensed how I felt, for the mischievous mood that I had learned to recognize and to love came over him as he said, 'At least, not yet, Roisin.' He flashed me a winning smile, his teeth very white in his tanned face. 'But soon, *mo mhuirnin*. Very soon.'

I couldn't resist his bright eyes, and I found myself forgiving him, telling myself that I was jumpy and imagining things, like any new bride.

The road followed the rough coastline of Kerry, through quaint villages with queer-sounding names. Just as my mother had told me, when I was a child, each of the small places had a history. Bren repeated some of the old stories to me, coaching me in my Irish as we progressed deeper into the Gaeltacht, where the old language is still spoken.

There was a misty quality to the air, which reminded me of San Francisco. An areola of clouds circled a large mountain looming near to the sea, in the distance, dominating a fingered, blue bay.

'Mount Brandon,' Bren said. 'With Brandon Bay shining below it.'

Bren swerved the small car without warning into a narrow, pale road that seemed hardly more than a trail winding between hawthorn hedges. The stiff branches grazed the flanks of the slim vehicle as we passed through.

'A shortcut,' Bren said.

It brought us near to the base of the mountain, which, Bren told me, had been St. Brendan's starting point, when he set out in 551 A.D. to discover what lay beyond the vast stretch of blue sea.

'Some say he was the first to discover the New World,' Bren said. 'He's the patron saint of this district.'

'And you are named for him,' I said.

He flashed me a beseeching look. 'Saint Brendan O'Leary,' he admitted. 'It's not often that I give it away. I suppose Father had some idea that it might influence me to follow the straight and narrow. At any rate, I'm stuck with it, and have been these twenty-odd years. To some, I suppose it might seem almost a sacrilege.'

'Because of your wicked ways,' I said, remembering our conversation on the plane.

I expected him to become mischievous, as he had then, leaning to kiss me, giving me the reassurance that I seemed so desperately to crave. Instead, his strange brows drew into a deep, dark V, and his handsome face clouded.

I said: 'Wicked or not, I still love you.'

His glowering expression didn't change, although he did steal a glance at me. His eyes were very bright and intense.

'Promise me that you shall never forget that,' he said. 'No matter what happens, Roisin.'

I have always taken the bright view of things. With Mother ill so much of the time, I had learned at an early age that it is the only way to triumph over despair. Perhaps that is why I refused to recognize the veiled warning behind his words. As though, I thought later, he had known all along that I would come to doubt him, and hoped to bind me with a promise.

Now I said dutifully, like any stricken schoolgirl: 'I promise.'

'I love you, Deirdre,' he said. His voice vibrated with emotion.

The world seemed suddenly to glow, and I looked out at it, marveling that he had such power over me. We had come to the base of the mountain, where, Bren told me, pilgrims still gathered in the spring, for the climb to the summit, on Saint Brendan's feast day. The remains of an oratory could still be found there at the top.

As he spoke, I wondered if he came to the mainland each May to join them, and I imagined his sturdy form there on the steep slope, leading them upward—King Leary, in his prime, striding forth with a certain, proud glory.

I thought, glowing innocently at the romantic notion: This is love, and nothing shall ever change it.

*   *   *

We came abruptly onto a plunging headland, and the road narrowed, becoming treacherous, as it swept above the blue bay. The sea expanded before us, and suddenly there was an island breaking its blue surface, just to the southwest of us, a tortured thrusting of mist-shrouded stone that bore a startling resemblance to the serrated spine of some

76

rearing sea monster.

A smaller island, showing faintly beyond the first, formed the monster's head, and I knew even before Bren told me that this was Inish Laoghaire, with Maguire Island just beyond.

Bren slowed the car, and I glimpsed the castle perched there against the dark stone. It looked like a child's toy. The island on which it stood seemed hardly more than a barren rock, cast into the sea by some gigantic hand, with no hint of a tree to relieve its austerity.

I had grown up with trees. Some of my disappointment must have shown in my face, for Bren said: 'Its entire aspect changes as we come nearer to it. You shall be duly impressed, Roisin, I promise you.'

'I am impressed now,' I said, swallowing my disappointment, consciously seeking some aspect of loveliness on which to comment.

I saw then the white wash about the base of the island—the massive churning of the surf against the cliffs. As the car sped on toward Kilmara, bringing us nearer to our destination, a lacing of pale stone walls appeared, covering the flanks of the island ridge. I glimpsed verdant patches inside the tiny squares.

'There are things growing there,' I said. 'Grass. But no trees?' I gave Bren a questioning look.

'If you want trees, my darling, there shall be trees,' he stated, flashing me an indulgent smile. 'Nothing shall be impossible now that you are back.'

'Back?' I gave him an amazed stare.

'You've always belonged here, you know,' he said. 'The little wild goose returned to the homeland.'

For an instant, I wondered if it was possible that he had forgotten that it had been Mother who was born in Ireland, and not me at all. But suddenly Kilmara appeared ahead of us, the most charming village I had ever seen, tucked into a cleft at the head of another bay—this one small and green, with strange, black boats bobbing on its surface.

'Curraghs!' I exclaimed.

Bren smiled at me, delighted that I had remembered.

*   *   *

At a small cottage in Kilmara, we met Bren's cousin Tim Donahue. He would be taking us out to the island, where he also lived.

I liked Tim Donahue at once. He was too much like Bren for me to feel otherwise. I stood looking into his gold-flecked eyes, which were slightly darker than Bren's, wondering suddenly what Bren's brother, Padraic, might be like.

Suddenly it seemed strange to me that Padraic hadn't come for us instead of Tim.

CHAPTER TWELVE

We had tea together in the cottage before we set out for Inish Laoghaire and Dunleary. A kettle swung over the open fire, boiling merrily, and I noticed that the cottage had been freshly cleaned and the walls whitewashed. The blue and brown striped mugs, hanging from the dresser, gleamed. On the scrubbed table, a fresh candle burned, glowing softly on the Brigid's cross which decorated the ceiling over our heads, sending out faint beeswax smells that mingled with the burnt hay aroma of the turf. The walls were decorated with holy pictures, and outside the window a Paul Scarlet rose bloomed in wild abandon.

I found it all very pleasant and cozy, and I found myself wishing that we might stay here, Bren and I; I wanted the cottage to be our home instead of the old castle that seemed so remote on its stark island.

I commented on the neatness of the cottage, and Tim seemed delighted.

'Sure I hoped you'd be pleased by it all,' he said.

I knew then that he was the one who had tidied it for my coming. I was touched.

'It's a comfortable place,' I said, to cover the sudden feeling that welled up in me. 'It would be pleasant to stay on here.'

'Dunleary is your home now,' Bren stated.

'God between you both and harm,' Tim said in a low, somber voice. It seemed almost to be a benediction that carried a solemn, dour undertone of warning.

Bren asked about things on the island then, and, as the two of them sat talking over their steaming mugs of tea, I pondered on Tim's words.

When we had finished our tea, Bren removed his jacket, and, in shirt sleeves, went to assist Tim with our luggage, which had to be transferred from the small car to one of the tiny, treacherous-seeming boats.

'We shan't be long, Roisin,' Tim said.

'I'll wait,' I smiled at him, aware that my face was flaming at his casual use of the familiar endearment.

'Sure you'll do,' Tim announced.

His clear, level eyes showed approval, and I wondered whether he was comparing me, favorably, to other women Bren had known and considered.

The two of them had no sooner gone than a knock sounded at the door of the cottage, and I opened it to find an old woman standing outside. She held a plate covered with snowy linen before her. I caught the mouth-watering aroma of freshly baked bread.

'God save all here,' she greeted me, her eyes frankly curious. 'May I be after coming in,

80

now?'

She told me then that she was Mrs. Callahan, from the cottage next door, and that from behind her curtains she had watched us drive up in Bren's small car.

'It is then that I said to meself: "the King is back," and, as luck would have it, I had just slipped a kettle of bread to bake beneath the turf.'

I asked her if she would like tea.

'Why else would I have come, now?' she retorted, settling herself firmly on a chair. 'And what do ye be called?' she demanded, as I took down a fresh mug and poured for her.

'I'm sorry,' I said, flustered by her intense scrutiny. 'I'm Deirdre. Deirdre Eileen ni Rynne, as you'd say here. Though it's O'Leary now.' I added quickly. 'Mrs. O'Leary.'

'The young Count's wife! Dear God bless your soul!' It was wondering, I was, what nature of woman The O'Leary was after bringing here, and I suspected the instant that I laid me eyes on you that you were one of us. Sure an egg wouldn't break beneath my feet now, for the gladness of my heart in hearing who you do be.' She leaned toward me, her eyes gleaming with some form of recognition. 'Where is it he found you now, darlin'?'

I told her that I was from San Francisco, and that before that I had lived in Ohio.

'Ohio, is it? Such a long way from the homeland for a young girl.' She shook her

81

head sadly. 'Although I understand there's monuments of money to be made there in America,' she added, brightening a little.

'I was born there,' I said. 'America is my homeland. That is, it was until now,' I added quickly.

'I should have guessed as much from the words in your mouth,' Mrs. Callahan said. 'It was the name that threw me off. Rynne. It's well known here.'

'My mother and father were Irish,' I said.

The old woman nodded, as though she had guessed as much before I spoke. 'How old do you be?' she demanded then.

'Nineteen,' I said.

'It's hardly more than a baby, you be, but old enough for a match, though most of us here wait until we're a good deal older to settle down,' she said, pausing to sip her tea. 'God between you and harm,' she added then, her voice tinged with a note of pessimism.

'Why does everyone here say that to me?' I demanded. 'As though there were some grave danger involved with marriage in this country.'

'Sure it's a risk you take when you're great for any man, though I'd say it takes more courage than most women possess to wed an O'Leary. It's because of the legend, dearie,' she added when I continued to stare at her, perplexed. 'Ach, now, don't tell me that you've not been after hearing it.'

'I don't believe in legends,' I stated.

'Sure others have said the same,' Mrs. Callahan said. 'The last who came here laughed at the curse. God help you, if you do be as frivolous as that one!'

'The last?' I felt suddenly apprehensive.

'A wild thing, she was. A foreigner. Eyes as black as berries, she had, and hair that gleamed like a crow's wing. There was an odd peak to it, now, pointing down between her brows.'

Katsy de Gomez, I thought, remembering Catherine's contrived widow's peak. A sense of eeriness and mystery came over me.

'Why did she come?' I asked.

'Who can say? A black, Spanish-looking woman, she was. It seemed a coincidence, at the time, a woman like that turning up at Dunleary.'

'Why should it have?' I asked, noticing that my hand trembled a little as I polished the mugs.

'Because of the legend, with its black curse, which was laid down by a Spaniard, dearie. Sure it was that strange.'

'I'm not familiar with the legend,' I admitted.

My heart had begun suddenly to pound. I fancied that I was on the verge of some dark, forbidden discovery.

'God help me, I thought everyone was after knowing that story,' Mrs. Callahan said, surprise showing in her blue eyes. It gave way at once, to something else, which I recognized as eagerness. 'It's after telling it all to you I'll be, if you've a mind to hear it,' she continued. 'It would be for your own good, darlin', since you are to live there on the island where it all took place.'

I nodded numbly, and the old woman rushed on, her eyes widening, in their pouches of wrinkled flesh, with a sort of horrified fascination at her own fast flow of words.

The story began with a Spanish ship that had once found its way into Inish Laoghaire's small, landlocked harbor.

'The ship was part of the Armada, which had set out from Spain in 1588 to claim England's throne for Philip II,' Mrs. Callahan said.

'A few of the ships were after making it to a safe harbor near the demesnes of the great Irish chiefs and lords, who recognized the black Spaniards as their allies against the greedy English, and sent them on their way with fresh water and supplies,' Mrs. Callahan continued. 'Sure the great galleon which wandered into the harbor at Inish Laoghaire was one of the fortunate few. It was after being captained by a man named De Medina.'

A sense of shock went through me at the name. De Medina! It had been the Condesa de Gomez's maiden name! I wondered if there could possibly be a connection. Intuition told me that there was.

'It's after being a handsome Latin the Spaniard no doubt was, for at once, The O'Leary's daughter, Maeve, was attracted to him,' Mrs. Callahan said. 'The two became keen for each other, and the Spanish captain swore that he would return to Inish Laoghaire after he had made his way back to Spain to report to King Philip, who had promised him a good deal of gold. The two were to be wed, then. However, The O'Leary wasn't keen for the red blood of the O'Learys to be diluted by this Spanish captain, and he arranged a match for Maeve with one of his handsome cousins. The two were married shortly before the Spanish captain's return.'

In spite of myself, I was caught up by the tale. 'Surely, if Maeve had truly loved the Spanish captain, she wouldn't have gone through with it,' I said.

'She had no choice, dearie,' Mrs. Callahan said. 'And Maeve herself ran down to the island's little harbor to greet Captain Juan de Medina when she saw his sails, and to inform him of her marriage to her father's cousin.' The old woman's voice became hardly more than a whisper. 'Ach, darlin', it was a nasty thing he did then. It is after ravaging her, he was, out of a strong sense of revenge— despoiling her for having betrayed him. And if that were not shame enough, he ordered his crew ashore, God save them, to have their way with those innocent island women.

'It was to a terrible scene of rape and pillage that the island men returned that evening, sounding their way through the heavy mist that lay low over the water. Sure the blood flowed on Inish Laoghaire, then, for the O'Learys were savage men by nature, and the Spaniards too besotted to run. Captain de Medina had broken out the tuns and casks of fine rum and wines, which he had brought with him to celebrate his marriage. It was after being an orgy they were having there, when The O'Leary and his men returned.'

'How terrible!' I gasped.

'Aye, they were insane with anger. They sunk the Spaniard's galleon somewhere there below the bare headlands.' Mrs. Callahan gestured through the cottage window toward the hump of island looming out of the blue sea, looking more darkly sinister than ever. 'It is said that there was a good deal of gold on it, intended as a wedding gift for Maeve.'

'Was it ever found?'

Mrs. Callahan shook her head. 'An ancient ducat or two washed onto the shingle here at Kilmara. No more.' She sighed, and continued with her story. 'The Irishmen set about killing the Spaniards at once, not stopping their slaughter until the last of them was dead. Sure they killed them all, including Captain de Medina, who cursed them with his dying breath.'

The old woman leaned close to me, her

86

words becoming almost sinister. 'God save them, the O'Learys have not known a moment's peace since that black day, for the curse cast by the Spaniard is with them still, there on their dreary island.'

'What was the curse?' I asked.

'"I damn your women to an eternity of wantonness and sin because of the one who betrayed me." Those are after being the Spaniard's exact words, uttered with his dying breath. So it was, dearie, with the women out there, and has been since. It's after being lustful, they are, and dying young for their trouble, as though the Lord and Saviour can't bear the sight of them chasing about after the men. Except, of course, for the one in white. Her name is Maeve, the same as the one who was keen on the Spanish captain. Although this one is not an O'Leary. A saint of some sort, they say she is, flitting about there in her long robes, making it up, no doubt, for all of the sinful women who have betrayed their men there on that black jutting stone.'

'It all happened so long ago,' I said.

'It was less than six months ago that the Spanish girl came here, asking to be rowed out to the island,' Mrs. Callahan stated.

I went to the window and looked across the blue water at Inish Laoghaire. A fog bank lay beyond it, hovering low over the sea, wisps of it breaking free, floating to shadow the island like a gray pall. A chilling sense of apprehension came over me.

'Why did she come here?' I asked.

'Who can say?' Mrs. Callahan shrugged. 'She was that odd. She refused to tell.'

'And she died there on the island,' I said.

'She was never seen again here on the mainland,' Mrs. Callahan told me. 'Nor has she been sighted through the glass for weeks,' she added, lowering her voice.

'You watch the island from here?' I asked, incredulous.

'What can be seen of it,' Mrs. Callahan said. 'Which is not a great deal, with the mist hovering over it nine days out of ten. Pat Mor, who owns the glass, once went to sea. He is elderly now, and tied to his chair these many years. It was a shark that did it—snatched away his legs. His keen observations through the glass have become his only source of pride.' The old woman gave a quick, excusing gesture. 'It was young like you be that she was,' she said, then, her eyes growing vague, and I knew that she was remembering Katsy de Gomez. 'Although her black eyes were after being as wise and crafty as an old woman's.'

'She lived there in the castle?' I asked.

'No one was ever certain,' Mrs. Callahan said. 'There is after being a good deal about that island that has never been explained. The O'Learys have always been close with their lives, and who can blame them? They are all affected by the legend there, though it happened ages ago.'

Mrs. Callahan scrutinized me carefully, her white head tilted a bit to one side. 'You've a sensible look about you, dearie, which is what it takes to get on there on the island. You'll not be like the rest of them, leading their unnatural lives. Sure there's that Maeve flitting about all in white. And the old Count,' she added, after a moment's hesitation. 'Sure he's gone queer, they say. Writes poetry and diddles a bit with the paints. Padraic, too, is affected. It is after being a collector of weird machines, he is. Terrible things they be, designed to torture men. God alone knows what he sees in them. They say he is after making lifelike figures out of wax to add to his display, though there is no one to see his collection.'

I thought, with a small, empty feeling of satisfaction, that I had been right: it had been Bren's brother, after all, who had purchased the De Gomez antiques. And because of them, Katsy de Gomez had come to Inish Laoghaire, hoping to have them back.

Had Padraic murdered her for her pains? I recalled Bren's apparent dislike for his brother. Was Padraic O'Leary a murderer? It shocked me to realize that I felt a sense of relief at the thought.

I had doubted Bren. I admitted it to myself now, feeling slightly ashamed. I went to the chair where he had tossed his jacket, and,

89

picking it up, I pressed the rough Donegal tweed against my cheek, breathing its comfortingly familiar aroma.

As I held it there, something fell from the pocket, fluttering to the flagstone floor. When I stooped to retrieve it, I recognized it as a clipping of some sort, taken from a newspaper. It had been creased into a small, tight square.

Innocently, I unfolded it, and saw my own face staring back at me, and beneath it, a black-lettered caption: *Deirdre Eileen Rynne, niece of San Francisco's Prominent Shipping Magnate, Connary Rynne.*

I realized that it was the story from the *Chronicle* announcing my debut with Catherine. It occurred to me that the article had appeared early in February, weeks before Bren had left Inish Laoghaire to come to San Francisco.

Numbly, I noticed that someone had doodled across the Roos Brothers ad, which appeared beside the picture. Bren, I thought, for the markings were distinct and bold—a jumble of hastily printed words absent-mindedly made to form a pyramid. I scanned them quickly before I refolded the clipping to tuck it carefully back into Bren's pocket. Startled, I realized that the jumble formed a message.

'Find out about this girl. Who is she? Where from? Family history. Background. Information before April 1' it read.

April 1st. The date of the ball, I thought, a chill going through me.

There were numbers scrawled heavily beneath the pyramid—the unmistakable numerals of Uncle Con's office address.

There was a frightening deliberation about the message. A cold tremor caused my hands to shake as I fumbled with the clipping, and I realized that it had not been chance that had brought Bren to Uncle Con's office the day Catherine had found him there—nor business.

Stunned, I thrust the clipping back into the pocket and laid his jacket back on the chair.

'Sure it will be a treat for the child there to have other youngsters joining him in his wild scrambles over the stony ridges.' Mrs. Callahan's persistent voice seemed to come to me from far away.

With difficulty, I picked up the thread of her thought. I glanced sharply at her.

'But there are no children there on the island,' I said. 'Only wild Irishmen and the elderly . . .' I quoted the hostess who had spoken to me at the airport, my voice trailing off.

'There is only the one child, dearie,' Mrs. Callahan said. 'A gossoon, tender in years. I've seen him myself, on a fair day, a small broth of a lad, seeking gulls' eggs on the cliffs.'

'Deirdre!'

I glanced up to see Bren watching us across

91

the half-door of the cottage, a look of displeasure darkening his handsome face. I wondered how much he had heard.

*　　*　　*

Bren and I walked in silence to the edge of the small bay, where Tim Donahue awaited us. As we passed by one of the freshly limed cottages, an elderly man was watching us from behind a glistening, small-paned window. I knew instinctively that it was Pat Mor, waiting to follow us with his glass.

'We'd best be on our way,' Tim said, when we reached him. 'The clouds are banked and I've no doubt that we're in for a bit of rough sea.'

I thought how gentle Tim seemed beside Bren, who waited, grim-faced, beside the slim curragh, to help me in. Remembering the newspaper clipping tucked into his jacket pocket, I hesitated for an instant. Then I thought: He is my husband, and for better or worse, I must go with him.

I reached out to him, aware that my hand was cold and trembling.

'Surely you've some other mode of transportation when the weather is foul.' My voice cracked.

It was Tim who smiled encouragement.

'We've a small steamer,' he assured me. 'For use to transport supplies and the livestock we raise there on the island. However, we've been known to float a horse ashore in a curragh.'

I looked incredulously at the light eight-foot boat, wondering whether or not to believe him.

The small boat dipped restlessly as Bren stepped into it, but neither of the two men seemed to notice.

Suddenly Bren cried out in a loud, ringing voice: 'Let's move her out, in the name of God!'

He jabbed the slim oars savagely, sending the small boat skittering over water that had become suddenly dark and ominous.

CHAPTER THIRTEEN

As we bobbed across that endless expanse of rolling sea, I felt that I had left the civilized world behind.

Dunleary, hopelessly medieval, loomed against the mist-shrouded sky, and as we drew near to it I recalled the frightening legend Mrs. Callahan had related to me.

I fancied that I caught the frantic cries of ravished women floating eerily over the writhing dark water, and, shivering, I pictured the dark, vengeful Spaniards set upon by the outraged Irishmen. The faint cries of infants seemed to come to me.

A shadow passed over us, and I glanced up

and saw that it was only a gull that I had heard.

I thought of the child Mrs. Callahan had seen gathering gulls' eggs on the precipitous black cliffs of Inish Laoghaire. Was there such a child? And if so, whose child was he? Bren's? The thought haunted me, and I found myself focusing my eyes on the island, as it loomed nearer, in an effort to distinguish the slight figure against the headlands that towered like great crannied walls out of the threshing water. It seemed impossible that anyone could cling to those rising scarps long enough to rob a nest.

The closer we came to the island, the more unreal it seemed. The limestone cliffs were eaten through by the wild seas, so that at close range it assumed the fantastic appearance of some monolithic cathedral surrounded by a maze of arches and pillars. Maguire Island, a frescoed vestibule, extended out from it to the south, its sea walls stained a dozen subtle shades by the sea.

There was no sign of a harbor along the rugged length of either island.

The sea had grown unbelievably rough but Bren was in his element. I saw it in his face, and found myself resenting his pleasure a little. Beads of spray stung my face and I tasted salt on my lips.

I must have looked frightened, for Tim called to me above the roar of the sea. 'There's no danger today, Roisin. Sure we're as safe as a newborn in its mother's arms.' His face was as calm and open as sunlight.

I tried to smile back at him, aware that Bren was watching me. His eyes squinted a little, so that they seemed to gleam like twin flames in his brown face. It occurred to me that he was displeased because I had given my attention to Tim. There was a wariness in Bren's eyes—an expression almost of distrust. I recalled the legend, with its black curse, and thought: Bren is very much affected by it.

He relinquished the long slender oars to Tim, and slid into place beside me. 'Deirdre,' he said beneath his breath, a warning note in his voice.

'I'm thinking that I should have brought the steamer, today,' Tim shouted, unaware of Bren's dark mood. 'Deirdre would have been more comfortable.'

'A little sea won't hurt her,' Bren shouted back, his face grim.

He reached possessively for my hand, his fingers closing around it in a painful grasp. I bit my lip to keep from crying out, and as we came nearer to the island, he seemed to relent a little, his face softening.

'The old woman annoyed me,' he said. 'I know her. She twists things to make them seem dramatic.'

I knew that it was the nearest he would come to an apology for his brooding, and I accepted it.

'I'm not one to be taken in,' I said.

'A virtue to please any king.' He gave me a slow, yielding smile. Then without warning, he pulled me to him and kissed me, tilting the boat dangerously.

'Curraghs weren't made for lovemaking,' Tim said dryly when Bren had released me. 'I've no taste for it myself, under these conditions. Not with those fellows hovering about.' He pointed into the water with one of the long oars.

Horrified, I glimpsed a sinister dark shape beneath the surface.

'Basking shark,' Bren said.

I thought of Pat Mor without any legs, and of something Bren had said to me in San Francisco when I had dared to suggest to him that I might not be the innocent he had imagined: *If I were to discover that you are a wanton, I would strangle you with my bare hands, and toss your body to the basking sharks off Inish Laoghaire . . .*

CHAPTER FOURTEEN

The curragh scraped onto the white sand of the small crescented beach and Bren leaped out, reaching for me. Tim steadied me as I moved forward in the small boat, his dark head bent toward me.

'Sure if things go wrong there at the castle, Roisin, come to me.' It was no more than a whisper breathed into my hair.

I glanced quickly at Tim, wondering if I had imagined the soft sound of his voice. His eyes, which had been laughing before, were darkly serious for an instant.

The wall of mist shifted restlessly over the island, as though it were stirred by some invisible hand, and I glimpsed sheep and cattle grazing high on the island ridge. I glanced up to see a tall man making his way down to us, his form outlined against the crenellated rise of Dunleary. There was something formidable about him.

'Padraic,' Bren said, all of the joy of homecoming going out of his voice.

I saw at once that Bren's brother was nothing like my husband, and recalled what Bren had told me of his brother's birth.

Padraic O'Leary was almost too beautiful to be a man. His skin was very fair and flawless, with a soft flush of color over his high cheekbones. His hair was an almost rosy shade of red rising above his face in satiny ripples and waves. His suit was dark and fashionable, contrasting sharply with the rough garb of the village men. An ascot of some exquisite fabric was draped softly into his open collar, picking up the vivid blue of his eyes. Yet for all of his exquisite coloring and beauty, Padraic was totally masculine, with a look of wiry strength

97

about his tall frame.

Bren introduced me to him, and Padraic studied me for an instant, giving me a knowing smile which I resented at once. 'Welcome to Dunleary, dear sister,' he said then, his voice deep and slightly hollow.

'Thank you,' I said coolly, something about him making me uneasy.

'Bren is most fortunate,' Padraic said, without feeling.

I fancied that had he been fierce, like Bren, the two would have been at one another's throats, for there was an unmistakable current of animosity between them.

'Where is Maeve?' Bren asked his brother.

A flutter of white caught my eye on the path above us, and a tall woman appeared, looking incredibly like Padraic. She stood regally for an instant on an outthrusting of stone, her white robe sweeping dramatically about her. The effect, against all of that stony ruggedness, was quite astonishing. I guessed that she had planned it to be.

'Here is Maeve now,' Padraic said, in his carefully controlled voice, which I realized was tinged subtly with acid.

I found myself wondering if Padraic were capable of benevolence beneath all of that exquisite masculine perfection.

Then I looked up to see Maeve moving toward us; she was a large woman, Amazon-like, and perfectly formed. Bren went forward

98

to greet her, and she stood quietly once more, allowing him to kiss her cheek.

Lot's wife, I thought, turned to salt. Then, as quickly as it had come, I banished the fleeting impression, remembering that Maeve was a saintly woman.

I couldn't help staring at her as she drew near. Her face was as smooth as a young girl's. It was only after I looked into her eyes that I could realize that she was a woman in her early fifties. Her hair, like Padraic's, was a rare shade of red, and she wore it bound around her head in a shimmering coronet, which had the startling effect of a halo. Like Padraic, she was extremely aloof and attractive.

Bren introduced us, and I imagined that I caught a flicker of displeasure on her smooth face. I couldn't be certain, for it vanished as quickly as it had come. Suddenly she smiled, a withdrawn and charming Mona Lisa smile, and I told myself that I was being foolishly suspicious of everyone because I was a stranger and new to the island.

'Welcome to Dunleary,' she said in a deep, soft voice.

She turned then and led us upward toward the castle. It occurred to me that she had been mistress here, and that now I would be taking her place. I wondered if the fleeting look of displeasure had not been real after all.

Padraic fell into step beside Maeve, looking back from time to time over his shoulder to speak to Bren.

'I'd have been there on the slip waiting for you if the old Count hadn't detained me,' he said. 'He has been terribly excited since we received the message telling us that you were on your way back to Inish Laoghaire with your new bride.'

His blue eyes shifted to my face.

'The old Count has composed an ode to you, my dear. He's waiting now in the castle, fully prepared to regale you with it the instant you set foot inside.'

'But that's charming,' I said.

'I'm afraid you don't quite understand,' Padraic said. 'Surely Bren has told you that the old Count is quite mad.'

I felt Bren stiffen beside me. 'You are exaggerating, Padraic,' he said sharply.

'*Am* I?' Padraic said, arching his red brows.

'I'm afraid he has grown much worse since you've been away, darling,' Maeve said to Bren in her soft, low voice, 'He's been anxious, you see, since we heard about . . . about your bride.'

Padraic gave me a cool smile.

'He was afraid that you might be dark-haired, like—' he broke off, flashing Bren a taunting look. 'Like Bren here, of course. The old Count favors auburn-haired women. He had to be certain that you were to his liking before he could complete his ode. He's been watching you through his telescope for the past half hour, bobbing about out there in the curragh.' He gestured vaguely toward the expanse of sea, which stretched between the island and the mainland. 'We spy on each other here, you see. It's our mode of self-preservation.'

'What an odd thing to say,' I said, feeling uneasy.

Was the old Count dangerous, perhaps?

'I shouldn't want anything to happen to you, dearest Deirdre,' Padraic said. 'This island is not the safest place in the world. For a woman,' he added.

'Padraic is speaking in riddles to confuse you,' Bren said. 'You needn't fear, darling. Now I've found you I shan't let any harm befall you.'

'How very touching,' Padraic said. 'I had no idea there was tenderness hidden there beneath your stony character, dear brother.' Padraic glanced at me. 'You've cast a spell over this savage brother of mine, Deirdre. Now I can almost picture him going balmy, like the old Count. Spouting poetry. Most astonishing.'

'One day I shall silence your evil tongue for good, Padraic,' Bren stated, squinting his bright eyes a little at his older brother.

Padraic laughed—a wicked, jarring sound. 'You daren't murder *me*, dear brother,' he said. 'I have Maeve and Deirdre here as witnesses to your threat.'

There was no missing the insinuation in Padraic's voice that Bren had murdered before. I thought at once of Katsy de Gomez.

'Don't forget that I am king of this island,' Bren stated, apparently unperturbed.

'You've been taken in by that archaic custom,' Padraic said in his blunt, hollow voice. 'It should please you to know, dear brother, that the old Count has completed a new volume in your absence. Another of his sticky testimonials to King Leary, and . . .' He paused, his gaze switching to me, roving unmercifully over my body. 'To his virgin bride, the tan-haired, freckle-faced enchantress.'

I cringed beneath his cold gaze, wishing suddenly that I could disappear.

'The old Count considers himself the Irish Shakespeare, dear,' Padraic said then. 'You shall soon discover for yourself the extent of the O'Leary madness.'

A muscle danced along Bren's jawline. He grasped my arm roughly and pulled me with him up the remainder of the steep trail.

Behind us, Padraic laughed.

CHAPTER FIFTEEN

We passed neat cottages with dooryards that were a tangle of bright flowers. I was trying to forget Padraic's dry, mocking laugh and so I asked which one of the cottages belonged to

Tim Donahue and his mother.

'They've a cottage back on the island,' Bren said. 'Aunt Sheila keeps to herself.'

'It seems that they would want to live at Dunleary with the rest of the family,' I said.

'She has her reasons for isolating herself,' Bren said.

We came to the top of the path, and the old castle stood forth—an indomitable arrangement of great gray towers and battlements. Dunleary had an air of arrogance about it. It seemed wedded to the rock on which it stood, as though it had been formed there in a past eon by some errant eruption of the elements.

'O'Learys have lived here for five hundred years,' Bren stated, his voice ringing.

In that moment, he seemed as unapproachably arrogant as the stony old castle before us.

He gave me an expectant glance and I said: 'I've never seen anything like it. It's overwhelming.'

The walls, dotted with narrow arched windows set deep into the raw stone, rose sheer above us. There seemed to be no doorway. The castle appeared to be as impregnable as the island. It straddled a crevice in the stone, and a small stream flowed from beneath it, following a tortuous channel toward the brink of the headland. A riotous growth of maidenhair fern feathered its rough edges.

'Medieval sanitation,' Padraic said, behind us. 'Would you believe, darling sister, that this innocent stream once served the castle latrines. The walls inside are hollow, with privy rooms for both men and women well spaced about the chilly great chambers straddling this pleasant rill.'

'Really, Padraic,' Maeve said, a look of disgust disturbing the porcelain composure of her face.

'I feel that I must warn our dear Deirdre of the hazards one runs into in a dreary old place like this, if she's to avoid a fall into the castle dungeon.'

'We've all the modern conveniences now,' Maeve told me. 'Thank goodness.'

'Our saintly Maeve avoids sackcloth and ashes,' Padraic said. 'Unlike most martyrs, she cherishes convenience.'

'Tell me how it was built,' I said to Bren, forcibly changing the subject. 'How did they bring all of these monstrous stones here to the island?'

'Sure it contains the best of the Irish stone,' Bren said, slipping into brogue. Emotion edged his voice, making it a bit rough. 'Marbles from the Angliharn and Gortachalla quarries near Menlo. And the black decorative stone and serpentinous marbles from Ballinahinch and Recess.'

'It seems impossible that they could have brought these monstrous stones from the mainland,' I said.

'God save us, they were men then,' Bren said. 'Sure I'd pattern myself on them, for they had great vigor and the courage to set out among the sharks, with their curraghs sinking to the brim from the weight of the stones.'

'I can see it in you,' I said. 'The strength to carry on, as they did.'

'For our sons,' he said softly. His voice vibrated around me, drawing me to him, and I forgot that I had doubted him in the curragh. 'One for each mile of this rugged island. It is six miles of it there be, and two wide, including Maguire Island.'

'But Maguire Island doesn't belong to you,' I said.

'It shall,' he stated. 'And when it does, I intend to populate it with O'Learys. You've the build for it, Roisin—for the making of fine sons, in spite of your slenderness.' The look of mischievousness that I loved came over his face. 'I'll take you onto the bog and teach you to catch turf like an island woman,' he added. 'It will give strength and endurance to your bones. Though we'll not spend all of our time with the turf.' He flashed me a sly smile.

'Is that why you've chosen me?' I asked, suddenly remembering the clipping folded into his pocket. 'Because I've the build to give you fine sons?'

'That among other things,' he said. 'The gardens are to the rear,' he added abruptly,

105

and I knew that he was evading me. He had no intention of telling me his true reason for having chosen me, Deirdre Rynne, from among all of the women he must have known.

'We enter Dunleary through the old monastery,' he told me. 'The chapel is there— the only part of the old ruin that we've bothered to restore.'

The small stream which ran beneath the castle tinkled merrily through the monastery ruins and past the tumbled remains of an ancient round tower, falling over pale limestone that was green and velvety with moss.

Maeve and Padraic followed us. I wondered how much of our conversation they had heard, and felt my face grow warm.

'I see you've discovered my garden,' Padraic said, and I realized then that the careless scattering of lush growth had been carefully contrived.

A cluster of large urns containing palm trees was visible through a stone archway, which led into a small courtyard. Padraic took my arm and led me toward them.

'My own small demesne,' he said. 'I've a gardener who tends it for me, of course—one of the men from the island village.'

Vivid flowers showered above us. I noticed that they were fuchsias. When I commented on their lushness, Padraic told me that fuchsias grew better on the Dingle Peninsula than anywhere else in Ireland, and that here on Inish Laoghaire they became even more profuse, shooting upward like trees. I remembered that Bren disliked fuchsias, and wondered if Padraic's garden were the reason he had compared them to wanton women.

'O'Learys created all of this,' Bren said behind us, ignoring Padraic's plantings. When I turned to him he indicated the length and breadth of the island. 'Including the soil in which Padraic's garden thrives,' he added, making it clear to us all that he did not include Padraic among the O'Learys.

'Part of it is O'Leary dust,' Padraic said, in a dry, unimpressed voice. 'O'Learys die like any other men.' He fluttered his hand toward a stone portico. 'The family burial grounds.'

I glimpsed a churchyard filled with graves, the stones crowding against each other with barely enough space left to walk between. To one side stood a smaller grouping of worn, moss-covered stones. I noticed a new, unmarked mound among them.

'The island women lie there,' Maeve said.

'Apart from the men, of course,' Padraic told me. 'Pure in death, if not in life.' He glanced at Bren, his eyes taunting again.

The antagonism between the two became almost stifling. I rushed forward, forcing a little cry of delight at the sight of the small stone chapel which stood at one side of the courtyard.

The tiny church had a steep slate roof, topped by a miniature tower. A short, plump priest emerged from the small building and hurried toward us, making the sign of the cross.

'Father Flaherty!' Bren went to receive the small man's blessing.

When my husband introduced us, I fancied that I glimpsed alarm in the priest's eyes, as though he imagined that he was admitting someone quite wicked to his small fold.

'God of virtues,' he said. 'It's happy I am to have you.' He spoke with solemn courtesy, his voice made musical by brogue. 'The old Count is inside the castle, waiting, and having a time of it, he is, to contain himself. You'd best hurry in.' He laid an imploring hand on my arm. 'Be patient now,' he warned. 'Sure it's only the *plamas* that can subdue him.'

I glanced helplessly at Bren, feeling suddenly frightened.

'It means soft talk, darling,' Bren told me.

*   *   *

Upon entering the castle, we stepped into a huge room which must have once served as the castle's great hall. The stone walls were draped with ancient tapestries.

I paused before an immense portrait of a fiery-eyed, dark-haired man. For an instant, I thought it was a painting of Bren.

108

'Leary the indomitable,' Padraic said, in his mocking voice. 'Leary, King.'

Ignoring his sarcastic words, Bren took my hand and led me toward a wide stone stairway.

'Is Padraic always like this?' I asked.

'Padraic was born with the devil's own tongue in his head,' Bren said.

Father Flaherty panted behind us up the broad, winding stairs.

'Faith, the old Count was there in the great hall waiting only seconds before you came,' he said. 'Dear God bless his soul, he's fled from his own son.' Then, in a guarded voice, 'Do you think it's wise, now, Bren, taking her to him when he's in a dither? Sure I could administer a powder. It's a fresh supply I have from Dr. Riordan on the mainland.'

I felt uneasy. 'He's sometimes violent, then?' I asked.

'You are jumping to conclusions, darling, because of what Padraic said,' Bren remarked through tight lips.

We came to a closed door. Bren knocked on it politely and then, with a sudden, impatient gesture, flung it wide.

A man—an older version of Bren—stood inside. He watched us with the same bright eyes set beneath dark winging brows—satanic brows that contrasted sharply with his white hair.

'Eevelleen!' he said, in a hoarse voice. 'Eevelleen!' He embraced me, and repeated

109

the endearment a third time.

When he released me, I glanced at Bren for reassurance. I thought that the old Count was quite mad, after all.

'Father, this is Deirdre,' Bren said in an even voice. 'Deirdre Eileen, my new bride.'

Some of the fire went out of the old Count's eyes, although they remained soft with an affection that baffled me. Astonishingly, the fear I had felt drained away, and I found myself suddenly drawn to him. I told myself that it was because he and Bren so closely resembled each other.

The old Count was a tall, neat man with freshly shaven face and thick white hair that was carefully combed. A long pinkish scar near his temple ran back into the white waves. What a terrible wound it must have been, I thought, and wondered how it had happened.

Plamas. I remembered the word Father Flaherty had used and said softly: 'Bren tells me that you write poetry. I understand that you have written something for me, and I should like very much to hear it.' I threw up my hands in a little imploring gesture. 'Please tell me what I may call you. I want us to be friends.'

'John,' he said. 'Surely you haven't forgotten, Roisin. I was christened John.'

'Bren neglected to tell me,' I said.

'But surely you knew.' The old Count gave me a quizzical look. 'And remembered,' he

110

added, in a sad, imploring voice.

'Your poem, Father,' Bren reminded him then.

'I'm no Yeats, you understand,' the old Count said, a pleased look coming onto his face. 'Though my heart is in my work, as his was.'

He picked up a sheaf of papers from a small table beside a deep chair and began to read in a low, resonant voice:

'The virgin of the isle has flown
And I am left to keep
My silent vigil here alone
Until death brings sweet sleep.

'Gone, long gone, is Eevelleen;
Sad am I who wait,
Hearing well the black gull's keen
At death's unyielding gate.

'Dunleary's rooftree echoed long
The wailing dirge of Leary, King.
Endless years of mournful song
From battered breast did ring.

'Until I saw her reappear
Once more upon that lonely place
Where Inish Laoghaire's sharp stones shear
The blue sea's raging face.

'The virgin maid once more was seen—

Eevelleen! I saw her there!
Freckled, tawny, little queen,
Her form yet young and fair.

'Returned, at last, my Eevelleen,
To Dunleary's shore
In answer to the black gull's keen,
Before death's yielding door.'

The old Count's hands began suddenly to
tremble. 'Eevelleen?' he asked in a piteous
voice. His eyes focused then in a suddenly
frightening stare. 'Forgive me, darling,' he
said. 'I know you so well. It's just that I can't
seem to recall your name . . .'

'Father, you've overtaxed yourself!' Bren
came quickly to him and led him, like a child,
to the chair.

'A powder, perhaps,' Father Flaherty said,
behind us.

Bren glanced at me over his shoulder. 'I
won't be long darling,' he dismissed me.
'Maeve will show you to our room.'

'Maeve?' The old Count murmured, staring
up at Bren with bright, questioning eyes. 'And
you, jackeen? Who might you be?'

I turned and fled out into the corridor.
Padraic was standing in the shadows a few feet
from me.

'What happened to make him this way?' I
demanded, still seeing the too-bright eyes that
had seemed so much like Bren's. 'He seemed

112

suddenly to forget . . . everything,' I ended lamely.

'I understand that it is quite often this way with the mad,' Padraic said rather smugly.

'But people don't just fall apart,' I insisted. I remembered the scar on the old Count's head.

'Not if it is congenital,' Padraic said. 'Some inborn defect of the mind.'

'Hereditary?'

'Precisely, dear Deirdre,' Padraic said. Then, condescendingly, 'I pity Bren.'

'But you are an O'Leary as well,' I snapped. Padraic held up a patient white hand. 'Surely my dear brother has filled you in on the family skeletons. The shameful circumstances of my birth, for instance. But I realize how much more fortunate I am than Bren. You see, dear Deirdre, not only do I bear a famous name and share the family wealth, but I have also been blessed with untainted blood. The healthy, homogenized corpuscles of some brawny fisherman, no doubt, while the O'Learys, God save them, have intermarried here on their precious island for generations, cousin to cousin. These old families are keen for keeping the strain pure. However, pure strains have a habit of going to seed. Yes, dear sister, I can hardly help feeling sorry for my blooded brother, and for you, sweet child.'

'But why?'

'Your children,' he said softly. 'Is there anything more sorrowful to a mother than to

113

bear an imperfect child? Bren is savage for children. You shan't avoid it, darling. And you've only to look at the old Count, as he is now . . .'

'Please!' I cried. 'I'm certain that our children shall be quite beautiful. Quite perfect, like Bren.'

'Is he so perfect?' Padraic asked.

Before I could reply, Maeve appeared at the far end of the dim corridor, her halo of bright hair seeming to glow softly.

I hurried toward her, thinking that I would avoid Padraic after this.

CHAPTER SIXTEEN

The room that Maeve took me to was large and chilly. Forlorn tapestries covered the walls here as they had in the great hall. A huge bed, swathed in a mass of dark hangings, stood on a raised dais in the center.

A maid, ancient like everything else inside Dunleary, was stoking up the turf fire as I entered. Her name was Bridget.

Someone had brought up our bags—Tim Donahue, I suspected. The maid bustled about with surprising alacrity when Maeve ordered her to begin unpacking.

I had tucked Mother's rosewood chest in at the last minute, and it was there on top of my clothing. Bridget lifted it out with careful hands.

'If you've anything of value in that,' Maeve said, lifting her brows at me, 'it belongs in the safe downstairs.'

'It's not the family jewels,' I said, forcing a smile. 'Only a few personal items that belonged to my mother. Nothing of value to anyone but myself.'

My wedding dress was there beneath the chest—a simple gown that Aunt Ruth had helped me choose. I explained to Maeve that I hoped to pass it down to a daughter of mine someday, as an heirloom. She gave me a disdaining smile.

'You'll want it put in the garret then. Bridget will attend to it.'

'Not just yet,' I said quickly. 'Perhaps there will be a party. It's really just a simple gown.'

'Whatever you wish,' Maeve said in a disinterested voice.

Bridget took the dress to a huge wardrobe.

Maeve soon left me alone with the ancient maid, who seemed terribly efficient in spite of her advanced age. When she had finished putting away the dress, she placed Mother's chest on a heavy dark table near the bed, hung away my frocks in the immense wardrobe, and stored undergarments in a tall dresser which looked as old as the castle, with its dark wood burnished by the oil from countless O'Leary hands.

I noticed that two heavy doors opened off the room. Thinking that I should know what was there, I tried them. The first, I discovered, opened into an amazingly modern dressing room, with a bath beyond. When I attempted the second of the two doors, I found that it was locked.

'You'd not be wanting to go in there, now, madame,' Bridget said. 'Sure it's nothing but the old privy chamber. There is one of those opening off of each of the castle's main chambers, though the men in those early days, God save them, relieved their bladders into the fire. It was uncivilized they were, then,' she added, her eyes twinkling. 'Forgive me, madame, for carrying on so, but it's good to be chatting with someone who has a youthful face to bless. It is glad I be to be the one chosen to look after you.'

'You're new here in the castle, then?'

'Aye. I came up the path yesterday with me things. It's a widow I be these many years, with my man long since laid to rest. My Lord and Saviour, it is good to be starting life over again.'

'Who asked you to come?' I said, suddenly curious.

'The O'Leary himself sent word from America, to Tim Donahue, that I was to be here when he arrived with his new bride.'

'I understand that another young woman came here recently,' I said, thinking suddenly

116

of Katsy de Gomez. 'A Spanish woman.'

'She's no longer here, madame,' Bridget said, avoiding my eyes and concentrating with a sudden intensity on a soft stack of lingerie.

'Where did she go' I asked.

'To the sea,' Bridget said.

'You mean that she left by curragh,' I said.

'Not exactly, madame,' Bridget said. 'Her body was found one morning, washed onto the rocks outside the mouth of the Spanish Cave, they say.'

'Was anyone with her when it happened?' I forced myself to ask, my voice trembling with some unnamed dread.

'She was alone, they *say*. Sure it was as though the dead there inside of the cave had reached forth to claim their own.'

'I don't understand,' I said.

'The bodies of the Spaniards, madame. Those who violated the island women on that bloody day long ago. The O'Leary ordered their bones tossed into the cave, where they were left to rot. Sure the skeletons can still be seen there.'

'It seems incredible,' I said, aghast. 'Where is this Spanish Cave? Is it near here?'

'There on Maguire Island, madame, across the small channel. There be only a stone's throw between the two islands. A part of Inish Laoghaire Maguire Island rightfully be. Though the sea has done its best to make it otherwise.'

'I understood that Maguire Island is owned by the Maguires,' I stated.

'So it is, with the last of the Maguires lying here in this gloomy castle. It is on the third floor she be, next to the old nursery. It is after bringing her here, the old Count was, to see to the young O'Leary when his mother died, and she has remained, poor woman, stricken down these many years, with no words left in her mouth.'

'It seems that those long-ago Maguires would have objected to having the dead Spaniards put into their cave,' I said, thinking with a little shudder that I must call on Mrs. Maguire. As the new mistress of Dunleary, it would be my duty.

'Aye, but there's a chance that the Spaniards brought a good deal of gold on their galleon. They were keen for gold, it is said. And a few coins have been found on the slip at Kilmara.'

'The Spanish Cave,' I mused.

I want no part of it, I thought. At the same time I wondered who had discovered Katsy de Gomez's body.

It occurred to me that Katsy de Gomez was becoming something of an obsession with me. I felt compelled to discover all I could about her. Only when I knew the facts, I thought, could I be entirely free from doubt.

'Why did the Spanish woman come here?'

'It would be worth my place here to say, madame,' Bridget said, her mouth puckering

118

unexpectedly into a grim line.

'Was it to see Padraic?' I insisted.

'The two were seen together about the island,' Bridget said carefully.

'I understand that Padraic collects antiques,' I persisted.

'That he does, God be good to him. I've seen his worthless instruments as they were being unloaded from the steamer. Frightful pieces of junk they be.'

'I've an idea he paid a good deal for them, junk or not,' I said.

'Ach, how could he have, madame, when they don't be worth the woodcock on a farthing. Padraic has no funds, everyone knows. 'The young Count is not a generous man when it comes to Padraic and, as you know, it is he who controls the purse. There is no love between the two of them.'

'Padraic looks prosperous enough,' I said. 'Well-dressed—'

'Sure every shilling he gets goes to cover his back,' Bridget said with a little gesture of disgust.

'I assume that the Spanish girl drowned,' I said.

Indecision flickered across Bridget's plump face. 'She was riding one of the steeplechasers when it happened,' she said cautiously. 'It is a dangerous trail the horses are accustomed to, following close to the rim of the island. It is believed that her horse became frightened and tossed her from the cliff into the sea. Sure it is a long way down to the angry water.'

'One of Count O'Leary's steeplechasers?' I asked.

'Sure there are no others,' Bridget said. And she started putting Bren's things away.

When Bridget asked if I wanted tea, I managed a nod. As she hurried toward the door, Maeve stepped into the room.

'I'll take tea with the Countess, Bridget,' Maeve said.

She turned to me when Bridget had gone. 'I couldn't help overhearing,' she said. 'I realize that you are terribly young and inexperienced, but you must understand at once that a lady does not fraternize with her servants.'

'I'm not accustomed to servants,' I stated.

'We've a staff of ten here at Dunleary,' Maeve told me. 'You shall find that the best policy with servants is simply to ignore them, unless of course one of them should become insubordinate. In which case, you have only to report to me.'

'I hope that I shall catch on very soon,' I said. I had become slightly defensive.

'It must have been a tremendous decision to make, marrying The O'Leary,' Maeve said. 'Knowing how it is with the old Count,' she went on. 'O'Learys have always been considered rather strange, living here as they do on this dreary island, shadowed by that evil curse. It has become an inborn trait for them to suspect women. I should be very careful if I were you, dear.'

'I find Bren quite fascinating,' I said stubbornly. 'So much so that I doubt that I shall ever stray away from him in search of whatever it might be that an unfaithful wife hopes to find.'

'Women have always been taken in by the O'Learys' black looks,' Maeve said. 'It is an unfortunate trait of the weaker sex that they are so often attracted to wickedness.'

'I have taken everything into consideration, and I am quite prepared to accept Bren just as he is. And his family,' I added, my voice breaking.

'Deirdre! I've upset you, dear,' Maeve came to hover over me, her soft voice humming. I felt her touch my shoulder, and the chill from her hand penetrated the thin fabric of my blouse. 'I'm sorry, dear; God forgive me. I had no intention of . . .' Her voice faded away for an instant. 'It's just that there are so many men here on the island, and so few women. I intended only to warn you.' She drifted toward one of the deep-set windows.

'Against Padraic?' I said.

'Padraic has nothing to do with it,' she said, her voice changing subtly.

'She followed him here, didn't she? Katsy de Gomez?' I said.

'Padraic didn't want her, of course,' Maeve stated. There was a definite tenseness to her

121

voice now. 'Padraic had done business with her mother in Spain. The Condesa de Gomez. It seems that the Condesa was a De Medina before her marriage—a descendant of the Spanish Captain who desecrated this island out of love for that first Maeve.'

'It was inexcusable,' I said.

Maeve flashed me a look, her eyes very bright and intense. 'Perhaps,' she said. 'But romantic, nevertheless. As I was saying, Padraic had business with this woman, the Condesa, and the girl, Katsy, took a fancy to him while he was there in Spain, completing his macabre little deal. She followed him here to Inish Laoghaire.'

'Padraic is very attractive,' I said.

'You are susceptible just as she was,' Maeve said, her blue eyes glinting suddenly with accusation. 'It's the curse, you know. It has already gained a hold on you before you've been twenty-four hours on this island!'

'I've no intention of betraying Bren with Padraic or anyone else,' I said. 'I have no faith in curses.'

'Foolish girl,' Maeve said, in her soft, powerful voice. 'The curse of the Spaniard is very real. All of your innocence and white wedding gowns won't help you now.'

I was stunned. Were her words a threat or a warning?

CHAPTER SEVENTEEN

Later, I ventured out into the hallway and stood hesitantly outside of the door to the old Count's room. Bren's voice came to me through the heavy panels, rising and falling in unmistakable rhythm. I realized that he was reading poetry. I huddled near the door, for some reason afraid to enter.

'Gone, long gone, is Eevelleen;
Sad am I who wait,
Hearing well the black gull's keen
At death's unyielding gate.'

The somber words came clearly to me. Through the tall, arched window, set deep into the stone at the far end of the corridor, I glimpsed gulls wheeling above the somber sea cliffs. I shuddered, wondering what the verse meant. Who was Eevelleen?

'You may as well accustom yourself to this sort of madness,' a voice said behind me.

I turned and there was Padraic again, quietly materializing from the shadows. I fancied that he had been waiting for me.

'You shall find that you will have a good deal of free time on your hands here at Dunleary,' he continued.

'I imagine that I shall discover ways to

occupy myself,' I said. 'I'm really quite resourceful.'

I glanced purposefully about the grim corridor, with its suits of ancient armor moldering beneath huge dark portraits of past O'Learys. I wondered fleetingly how one kept house in such a dwelling.

'Perhaps you shall discover ways to include me in your little plans,' Padraic said. 'I should be terribly grateful to you, little sister, if you were to take it upon yourself to alleviate my extreme boredom from time to time. My dear brother insists upon maintaining a state of isolation here as though we were a colony of lepers! Man the stronghold! Keep out the invaders! While in reality we could use an invasion here. Man the steamer, I say. Bring the tourists across the channel by the hundreds, with their fat little purses, not to mention their eager women.

'This place could be quite rewarding if Bren would only listen to sense. Consider what the blue bloods of England have done, opening their feudal homes to touring parties for a fine, fat fee. Those ancient old strongholds have suddenly evolved into a natural resource. A little development . . .' He gestured broadly.

'But it would be spoiled, then,' I said. 'Like the American forests when they put the freeways through. There would be beer cans scattered about your lovely garden, not to mention gum wrappers and things. Now, it's as a castle should be a little frightening, with its ghosts from the past hovering about—'

'And you are quite genuinely frightened by it all,' Padraic said. Then, in a soft, subtle voice: 'And you should be, my dear. You see, that is part of Dunleary's charm. The legend, with its remarkable curse, is all quite real. You see, there have been any number of hapless victims right here at Dunleary. You have only to visit the churchyard to find them. The fallen women of Dunleary, all of them wives to The O'Leary.'

'But what happened to all of the wives?' I asked.

'O'Leary women are accident-prone, darling. Perhaps it is the curse.' An expression of amusement came over Padraic's even features. 'I advise you to visit the churchyard. You might find it extremely enlightening. In the meantime, I find your girlish innocence quite charming.' He cocked his head speculatively to one side. 'You are really a good deal like her, you know,' he said then. 'Of course, knowing Bren as I do, I expected that you would be.'

'Like whom?' I demanded, feeling suddenly cold.

'Surely Bren has told you of his one and only true love,' Padraic said. 'Warned you that you would be competing.'

I stood there stunned, not quite comprehending what he had said.

'I see that my brother has kept his past to himself,' Padraic said with a maddening smile.

'Who is she?' I asked, my voice hardly more than a whisper. Was Katsy de Gomez still alive, after all, somewhere inside the dreary old castle?

'Her name was Eileen,' Padraic said. 'She's been dead for twenty years. Or so we here at Dunleary have been led to believe.' He moved nearer to me, his blue eyes suddenly accusing. 'Now that I've seen you, I'm not at all certain that she actually died.'

'Bren would have been only a child,' I said, staring up at Padraic in disbelief.

What was he trying to tell me, with his cold, accusing eyes? I shrank back from him, repelled.

'A somewhat precocious child, I fear,' he said. 'Eileen Maguire was years older than Bren—true. But the difference in their ages hardly kept them apart. They were together constantly, roaming about the island like wild sheep. Bren never got over that foolish childhood infatuation. Perhaps because the old Count has kept Eileen alive for him all of these years with his mad poetic fantasies. I've suspected for some time that my brother was becoming obsessed by our father's romantic ramblings.'

'Bren loves me,' I said, without conviction.

I thought of the newspaper clipping. It seemed more than coincidence that I should

126

be tawny and freckled, and that a part of my name should be the same as that of the girl Bren had adored as a child.

'You are naive, my dear,' Padraic said, his voice patiently amused. 'Bren has been in love with a vision for twenty years. You happen to fit the rosy picture of virginal womanhood that the old Count has painted for him with his insane verse. You see, dear, Bren is not actually in love with a real girl at all.'

'But that's absurd,' I protested. Yet it was not quite so easy to dismiss all that Padraic had said.

'Absurd or not, it happens to be the truth,' Padraic said. 'He has been subjected to the old Count's verses these past twenty years. You've no idea how sweet and pure our dear father has made Eileen out to be. Eevelleen, he called her. You see, he loved her, too, and between the two of them, they have idealized her beyond recognition. As though Eileen Maguire were the only virgin ever to be born into this wicked world.'

Padraic's eyes burned nakedly in his smooth face. Without warning, he leaned toward me and his warm, moist lips brushed my cheek. Repulsed, I turned and fled.

His laugh followed me—a hollow, mocking sort of mirth, like the evil chortle of some brightly lascivious bird.

*   *   *

I lay with dry, staring eyes in the big bed, wondering if now that we had arrived at Dunleary, Bren had deserted me for the tan-haired, freckled Eevelleen of the old Count's poetry.

Naively, I had imagined that we would be together a good deal at Dunleary, waking and sleeping. Now I realized that it wasn't to be that way at all—that I must share Bren not only with his ailing father but with some fox-haired creature from the past, whom I had never seen.

Eileen Maguire. I tried to picture her, and visualized myself. It occurred to me that Mother's name had been Eileen. Eileen Maginnis. I was struck by the similarity between the two names. Maginnis. Maguire. Suddenly my heart began to race. Had it been Mother Bren had loved? Was she the Eevelleen of the old Count's poetry? Had Mother loved Bren as a child, and did that in some indescribable way explain why I had been so helplessly attracted to him?

I lay very still, stunned by these incredible thoughts.

It was late when Bren finally slipped into our room. He stood for a moment silhouetted against the dim light which burned in the corridor outside, seeming taller than life.

'Deirdre!' His voice was harsh.

I realized that he was, for some

128

unaccountable reason, furious with me. Padraic's strange words came flooding back, and I cringed into my pillow, my eyes growing moist with tears of betrayal and frustration.

'I know all about it!' I lashed out. 'I know now why you chose me to be your bride.'

He was beside me in an instant, his eyes sparking in the half-light.

'Deirdre, in God's name, what are you saying?' His eyes were fiery, but there was no conviction in his voice.

'Padraic told me about Eileen Maguire,' I said. 'And your childhood infatuation with her. He suspects that you've brought me here on the strength—'

'The curse of Cromwell on Padraic!' Bren spat, and again his voice lacked depth. I fancied that for some reason he was relieved.

'Padraic has the devil's own tongue in his head,' he continued. 'You'll not be listening to his wild talk, Roisin. Is that understood?' He gripped me by the shoulders and pulled me against his hard body, his fingers biting through my thin gown.

'What else did Padraic say?' he demanded. 'What else did my precious brother tell you?'

'That you were always with her as a boy,' I said. 'That you have never forgotten her in all of these years, and that I am very much like her—so much so that he can hardly believe that she actually died.' I shuddered, as though I were cold.

129

'Did he touch you?' Bren demanded. 'Did Padraic put his hands on you?'

'No!' I said. I remembered the expression that had been in Padraic's eyes and the touch of his moist mouth on my cheek. 'No!' I repeated with vehemence, as though by denying it it could be erased.

'I'm angry with you simply because you haven't sense enough to lock your door,' Bren said.

'Because of Padraic?'

'I don't know.' He seemed suddenly tired. 'I don't know, Roisin.'

'What is it?' I felt uneasy.

'Strange things have happened here at Dunleary, darling. I should have warned you sooner. This is not a normal household. Far from it, I fear. It's not just Father's precarious state of mind . . .'

'It's the legend, isn't it?' I said, in a dull, hopeless voice. 'It's because all of you here are still affected by it.'

'Yes, Roisin, I admit quite freely that I am affected by the legend—that we all are here. However, it requires a human element to perpetuate a legend such as ours, to keep it alive through the years.'

'And someone here at Dunleary has done that?' I asked in a hoarse whisper.

'I've suspected it for some time. As my bride, you shall be subjected to all sorts of . . . I must warn you, darling . . . I almost wish that I hadn't brought you here to the island. If you were to be violated. Harmed . . .'

He pulled me against his hard body once more with unmerciful strength, crushing the breath from me. His voice rumbled into my hair.

'I'll stop short of nothing to destroy that evil legend. I grew up under the unspeakable shadow of that wild tale with its godless curse. I'll not have our sons' lives affected by it, as my own has been.' He paused for an instant, and when he spoke again, his voice was sad. 'And Father . . . Look at him—what is left of the man he once was. It's time the legend died, and the curse with it.'

'But if someone here has been perpetuating it all these years, as you say, by making it all come true over and over again . . .' I broke off, sickened by a sudden thought.

It would have to be someone old. Someone like the old Count.

'I shall kill whoever it is.' Bren spoke very calmly.

I looked into his face, telling myself that he didn't mean it literally—that he was upset because of the things Padraic had said to me.

Sensing my withdrawal, he tilted my face, and kissed me. It was a passionate kiss that swept me away, for the moment, miraculously blotting out fear.

CHAPTER EIGHTEEN

The following day, which turned out to be quite glorious, with not even a hint of mist lingering on the horizon, was overshadowed by a strange and rather frightening occurrence. While Bren and I were at breakfast in the large dining room, someone had entered our room and slashed my wedding dress.

I returned to my room after Bren had left me to attend to duties outside the castle, to find Bridget hovering over the gown, which had been torn from its hanger in the wardrobe.

'Whoever could have done a thing like this?' I cried, when Bridget held forth the soft folds, which had been shredded by some sharp instrument. There would be no cherished heirloom, laid away in some upper chamber of the castle, as I had envisioned.

Bridget gave me a hesitant look.

'Did you see who it was?' I demanded, something in her eyes prompting me.

'Sure it was a man, madame, and him fleeing before me like a sedge rabbit as I came through the door just now,' she said.

'Did you recognize him?'

Bridget lowered her voice. 'I'm thinking it did be the old Count. He is after wandering a bit, madame, take it from me who knows. I'd not be wanting to tattle on him, now. The young Count has enough on his mind, as it is, God save them both.'

I remembered the kindness I had glimpsed in Bren's father's eyes.

'I can't believe the old Count would do a thing like this,' I said. 'The O'Leary told me that his father is really quite harmless.'

'Not in his right mind he wouldn't, madame, for he was always kind. It is his affliction that has made him strange. Sure he went into there, he did.' Bridget pointed toward the old privy chamber.

'It's locked,' I said.

'Then he did be a ghost, God save me, for that is where he disappeared to.'

I approached the privy room door, my heart pounding with an unfathomable sense of dread. I tried it with shaking hands.

To my surprise, it swung open to reveal the small, dark room. The latrine cover—a heavy tapestry-covered plank, faded and dusty with age—stood open. Tentatively, I peered down into the bottomless depths of the old castle and heard the small stream trickling eerily below—the sound magnified by the great hollow walls. Modern plumbing had been installed in the narrow spaces between the huge stones. A chill went through me as I realized that the black pipes, dripping with moisture, formed a precarious ladder that would give access to privy chambers all over the castle.

As I stood leaning over the gaping pit, a new sound wafted up from below. I realized that it was a harsh whisper, magnified like the splashing sounds of the water.

'Gone, long gone, my Eevelleen;
Sad am I who wait,
Hearing well the black gull's keen
At death's unyielding gate.

'Returned, at last, my Eevelleen,
To Dunleary's shore
In answer to the black gull's keen
Before death's yielding door.'

'Why, madame, it is as white as a ghost that you be,' Bridget said, rushing to steady me with a work-gnarled hand.

'Whoever it was is still there,' I said, in a trembling voice.

I drew a deep breath and attempted to regain my composure.

'Sure he got away into that stinking pit; the door being unlocked now proves it,' Bridget said. 'God and yourself willing, madame, I'll go to fetch The O'Leary, as I should have done when I first suspected the old Count was rummaging about. It's a powder he's after needing when he do be like this.'

'No!' I said sharply. Then in a more gentle voice: 'It's too late to save the dress.'

'But your things—them that is in the little

chest.'

I noticed then that Mother's rosewood chest had been removed from the bedside table. Whoever had been in the room had obviously taken it. Yet it seemed impossible that anyone could have made their way down through the ancient walls of the castle saddled by that extra burden, small as it was. Both hands would have been needed to negotiate that endless array of slimy black pipes, I thought, unless that person were terribly strong. The old Count had seemed quite frail.

Hurrying into the privy chamber once more, I searched about quickly and found the chest toppled into a dark corner. I opened it and lifted out the old rosary, then the garnet earrings, and the amber beads. The small book of poetry, with its dried cluster of flowers, lay underneath. When I lifted it out, the flowers fell from between the pages with a crisp little rustle. Bridget reached down to retrieve them.

'Sure it's bog cotton tassels they're after being,' she exclaimed. 'And all turned brown.'

I suddenly recalled Bren's odd simile the day we had lunched at Cliff House, and the flowers took on a special significance. I carefully put them back into the book.

'It's because you remind him of *her*,' the ancient maid was saying. 'The one he is after writing all of those poems about. Sure I can see now why he's slipped into here to slash your wedding dress. It's after wanting her for

135

himself he has been these many years, and no sense to it, God save him, for she is dead.'

'Eevelleen?'

'The same,' Bridget said. 'It was a pet name he had for Mrs. Maguire's daughter, Eileen. Sure the whole island was after knowing how keen he was to make a match with her, though she was after being years younger than himself, and him with white hairs sprouting already on his head. But a fine man he was, and his mind still sound then.'

'Did you know her? Eileen?'

'Did I know her? Do I know my own old red petticoat? Aye I knew her as well as I know bread.'

'What was she like? I'd really like to know.'

'My Lord and Savior, it was after being like yourself she was, of course. That same speckled skin, and eyes the tawny color of a fox's pelt. Her hair was a mite longer than your own do be, I am thinking, but the shade was the same.'

'What happened to her?' I clutched the small book tightly to keep my hands from trembling.

'She died young. Twenty or more years back, it was. The young Count was a wee gossoon. To be sure, she was only nineteen. A virgin still, they say, for all of the black Spanish curse hanging over the island.' Bridget broke off, her faded eyes focusing suddenly on me. 'And now you do be here, and the old Count has become confused as to your true identity. Sure that is all the torn dress amounts to. God between you and harm, madame, it could have been a good deal worse.'

CHAPTER NINETEEN

I began my duties as mistress of Dunleary by paying a call on Mrs. Maguire in her third-floor room, which was located next to the old nursery where Bren had slept as a child. Because Mrs. Maguire had been Bren's nurse and because she had been Eileen Maguire's mother, I felt an eagerness and curiosity about her.

A long, narrow window lighted the third-floor landing, and I paused for a moment before it; I gazed out across the stone-laced expanse of Inish Laoghaire, and Maguire Island, which was barely visible, beyond. A flutter of white caught my eye. Maeve, I thought. A second later, two figures emerged from behind a wild upthrusting of wind-worn stone, and for an instant I imagined that she was with Bren. Then I realized that the man with Maeve was Tim Donahue. The two of them walked very close, so that Maeve's flowing robe, teased by the breeze, entrapped Tim's legs. He stooped to unwind it, and as he did so, Maeve threw back her head, her fabulous halo of red hair glistening in the sun. There was something unrestrained in the gesture, and I guessed that she was laughing.

Puzzled, I turned from them to scan the length of the island to the north of the castle. A rider appeared, following the path along the brink of the cliffs. It was Bren, who looked superb, even at that distance, in his dark riding clothes and gleaming boots. As I watched, he wheeled his horse suddenly, so that the sleek animal seemed, for a frightening instant, almost to glide through empty blue space. The shining steeplechaser stretched its incredibly long legs and leaped over one of the high stone fences in a single bound.

As I turned my gaze back toward the village, I felt grateful that he hadn't persisted in giving up his horses, for he and the gleaming mount seemed to complement each other. I saw then that Tim and Maeve had disappeared, and it occurred to me that it was merest chance that had brought them into view for an instant. The southern portion of the island was composed of careless juttings of worn limestone. I tried to imagine what the two of them were doing there, and remembered that Tim and his mother had a cottage somewhere on the far side of the island, away from the village.

Mrs. Maguire lay in a high, bolstered bed that was set against one of the tall arched windows in the room. From the window there was a view of the strip of cornflower sea that separated Inish Laoghaire from the mainland. The jaunty little cluster that constituted Kilmara was visible in the distance, and I thought of Pat Mor and his glass.

A large-boned woman, with a long, angular face, watched over the stricken woman. She told me that her name was Mrs. Kelly and that she had been with the O'Learys for a good many years.

'It pleases her to watch The O'Leary astride his steeplechasers,' Mrs. Kelly told me, pointing to the window. 'Sure you must be proud, fine-looking man that he is. You will understand her fascination when I tell you that Mr. Maguire once worked here on Inish Laoghaire as a trainer of the O'Leary horses.'

My mother's father had been a horse trainer. The thought struck me with shattering force, and I clutched at the foot of the bed to support myself.

A cunning look came onto Mrs. Kelly's face.

'Ah, now dearie, there you are,' she said, leading me firmly to a chair. 'You can't keep a thing like this from a nurse, you know. Sure you must be proud to find yourself caught so soon.'

It occurred to me that she thought me pregnant, and I made a feeble protest.

Mrs. Maguire was watching me, her eyes like burnt holes in her sagging face. I imagined that I detected recognition in them, and I went over to her and took her hand. I was on the verge of speaking to Mrs. Maguire, when Mrs. Kelly came to fuss over her; she took away the pillows and lowered the old woman's limp head.

'It was kind of you to come up,' Mrs. Kelly said. 'She has no family of her own. There is only herself, lying here the same as dead these many years. God bless her dear soul, it would be a mercy if he saw fit to carry her off.'

'No!' I protested. Mrs. Kelly gave me a curious look. 'It's just that everyone has a right to live out their life . . .' Then I added quickly, lest I betray my suspicions, 'How long has she been like this?'

'Since the old Count was stricken. It would be twenty years now, I believe. Faith, time flies as though it were a bird with wings.'

'There was some connection between the old Count's sickness and this woman's stroke?'

'It was coincidence, they say, that both of them were struck down, though you could hardly call the old Count's misfortune a stroke.' Mrs. Kelly's voice swelled with importance. 'In strictest medical terms, we call it trauma. Dr. Riordan on the mainland will confirm my diagnosis, I am certain.'

I told Mrs. Kelly that she seemed to know a good deal about medicine, and that I could tell by Mrs. Maguire's appearance that she took excellent care of her patient. The nurse seemed terribly pleased and shifted Mrs. Maguire's position a bit in the big bed.

140

'Bed sores, you know, dearie. How they fester once they get a start. I change her position frequently.'

It occurred to me that Mrs. Kelly was in a position to know a good deal about what took place at Dunleary, and I said, with deliberate cunning: 'Although there is nothing definite yet, the Count wants a good many children. I hope that I shall soon give him a son.'

'God love you, you're hardly more than a child yourself,' Mrs. Kelly said. Her eyes, which were a lively shade of brown, took on sparkle in her creviced face. 'When the time arrives, you shall be needing advice from someone in the profession.'

'I'd hoped you would be willing to tell me anything that I might need to know,' I said. 'I know nothing about having babies.'

Nothing could have pleased her more than this new possibility in her lonely life. She fussed over me, making me sit on a comfortable chair, and I told her that I wanted to learn as much as possible about Dunleary.

'There has been no heir born inside this gloomy castle since the young Count himself was an infant,' she said. 'He will be beside himself when you've news for him.'

She gestured subtly toward Mrs. Maguire. 'This one, God give her rest, knows what it is to die without an heir, and as though that weren't pain enough, there are the two of them hovering about like vultures, with paper and pen in their hands. It is after her island, they are,' she added.

'But who would want Maguire Island?' I said. 'It hardly appears to be habitable, with all that rough stone.'

'Maeve and Padraic,' Mrs. Kelly said. 'Maeve has some scheme to establish a cloister there—an order, you might say. And Padraic makes a great thing of bringing the tourists out to the island.'

'They want to buy it from Mrs. Maguire?'

'They've not got enough money between the two of them to buy string. It's a lease they have in mind. Though of course the two of us know that nothing can ever come of it.'

'I've no idea what you mean,' I said.

Mrs. Kelly tossed me a little leer and her face became suddenly smug. 'The young Count was overheard, just before he left for America, telling Padraic that Maguire Island was the same as his own.'

I thought of the clipping that had fallen from Bren's jacket pocket; the pyramid of words penciled on the Roos Brother's ad loomed large in my mind. *Find out about this girl. Who is she. Where from. Family history. Background.*

Had Bren discovered what I myself suspected—that my mother had been Eileen Maguire? Had he married me because I would inherit Maguire Island? I pushed the preposterous thought from my mind.

I asked about the old Count. 'You mentioned trauma,' I said. 'I'm afraid that as a mere layman, I hardly understand.'

'It was an accident that laid him low,' Mrs. Kelly said. 'I attended the wound myself, until Dr. Riordan could be summoned from the mainland. Padraic, it was, who found the old Count lying below the headland on the rocks. It was his head, laid open as neat as you please. I've seen that nature of wound, in my younger days, when I was a nurse in Dublin, where they've many a rowdy pub.'

'Did they find out who struck him?'

'It was only the stones, after all,' Mrs. Kelly said, her face thoughtful. 'Padraic was there and had seen it. And Maeve and Mrs. Maguire as well, although this poor woman was unable to add her say. Padraic and Maeve stuck together on the story.'

'But you had your doubts,' I said.

'I had my professional opinion,' Mrs. Kelly said. 'Dr. Riordan agreed with me that it was an unusual wound to have come from a fall onto the stones. You've seen the scar?'

I nodded.

'The fall affected his mind,' Mrs. Kelly told me. 'He has no memory of the accident. There are times when his ramblings grow wild. Sure the things he says then would draw the devil himself.'

There was a small movement on the bed. I glanced over to see Mrs. Maguire watching me, her eyes seeming to glow in her pasty face. I fancied that they flashed me a plea for understanding.

'What is it?' I asked, going to stand over her. 'What is it that you are trying to tell me?'

I glanced helplessly at Mrs. Kelly. 'Please,' I said. 'She is trying to tell me something. I'm certain of it.'

I realized that my heart was thudding with some monstrous anticipation, and that I was quite out of breath.

Mrs. Kelly gave me a curious look. 'No doubt you remind her of her daughter,' she said. 'Eileen looked a good deal as you do.'

'Her daughter must have died shortly before she had the stroke,' I said.

'Aye, a tragedy it is that Eileen Maguire should have fallen into the sea and drowned the very day that her mother was struck down. She was that fond of walking on the cliffs above the wild ocean, and it had happened before, on Inish Laoghaire.'

'My mother's name was Eileen,' I said. 'She named me for herself. Deirdre Eileen.'

The woman on the bed made a convulsive movement.

'All of this talk has upset her,' Mrs. Kelly said. 'It is easy to forget that she has ears.'

She went to the bed and adjusted Mrs. Maguire's pillows once more, speaking to me over her shoulder.

'Deirdre Eileen, you say, and an odd

coincidence it is, for you do look a good deal like her, which may be why the young Count found himself attracted to you.'

'If Eileen Maguire hadn't drowned, I might almost believe that I had solved my mother's past,' I said.

'Her body was never found.'

'Do you suppose—?' My heart thudded with a quick rush of excitement.

'Sure she was a good girl. She wouldn't have left her mother,' Mrs. Kelly said.

I looked at the old woman in the bed. Are you my grandmother, I wanted to ask. Do you know the secret of my mother's past?

I said, 'I'm sorry if I've upset you, Mrs. Maguire.'

I turned to go. I must suddenly have looked ill, for Mrs. Kelly became very professional; she lay a hand on my forehead and felt for my pulse with the other. I assured her that I was fine, and escaped from her groping fingers, and the burning eyes that peered up at me from the bed. They seemed, I thought, suddenly hopeful.

CHAPTER TWENTY

Little by little I explored Dunleary, and perhaps because of what Padraic had said about the churchyard, the plot of graves on the slope behind the small stone citadel seemed to draw me.

This day, I gave in to the morbid urge which had been with me for the past week, and went deliberately to the churchyard, where I wandered about aimlessly among the graves. It seemed like any ordinary cemetery, except that the graves were closer together—probably to save precious space, I thought. I stooped to read the epitaphs carved into the crude stone markers.

After a while, Father Flaherty emerged from the small abbey to join me, and the two of us strolled together.

'Are the island men and women still buried apart, as they were in the old days?' I asked, going toward a small cluster of stones where Maeve had told me that the island women lay.

'Aye,' Father Flaherty said. 'God save us, the proprieties must be kept, even in death.'

'Is it because of the curse?' I asked.

'It is custom, child,' Father Flaherty said. Then, he pointed to a flower-smothered grave: 'That is the old Count's first wife. She is long dead, God be good to her.'

'Padraic's mother?'

'Aye.'

'How did she die?'

'Fell down the stair, she did. She had gone up to the nursery to see Padraic, who was only an infant then. The women were after wearing their skirts long in those days, and she tripped, so the story goes, and struck her head on the stones.'

'And the others? I suppose that they are all buried here. All of the old Count's wives. Bren's mother. And there were two others before her, I understand.'

'The old Count has had no luck with women,' Father Flaherty said. 'Bren's mother died in her bed. Childbed fever, Dr. Riordan was after calling her affliction. He is a conscientious man, take it from me who knows. Nevertheless the fever set in.'

'Perhaps the nurse . . . Perhaps she wasn't careful.'

'Ach, child, it was after being Mrs. Kelly, and Maeve attended to her through the wee black hours of the night.'

'And the wife before her?'

'Wandered into one of the old privy chambers, and tumbled to her death down the latrine.'

'How horrible!'

'God's will,' Father Flaherty said. 'She was seeking a way to utilize the old privy rooms. God knows what scheme she had in mind when she went crawling about those dangerous holes.'

'There was one more,' I said.

'It was a painful death that took her off. Charred, she was, by the flames.'

'She was burned to death?'

'Sure the old Count was away from the

island at the time. It was after being a freezing night. Poor soul, she had risen from her bed and backed up to the open fire to warm herself. Her gown burst into flames.'

'But couldn't someone have helped her? Tossed a rug about her? Put it out?'

'It was a gown made of new flannel, which exploded as though it had been soaked in petrol. The woman was after being a living torch.'

'The old Count has had his share of troubles,' I said.

'He has that, and all for the want of a woman to warm his bed.'

A little shudder of horror swept over me. I saw that a monument had been erected over the fresh mound of earth that I had noticed that first day at Dunleary, and I went toward it. The native stone had been intricately carved, with a design of cherubs wafting garlands of stone roses about its raw edges.

'It was there this very morning,' Father Flaherty said of the new marker.

'But it's exquisite,' I said, bending to examine it. 'However, there seems to be no legend.'

'You don't know who lies there, child?' he asked.

'No. Should I?' Then, 'This is my first visit here to the churchyard. I've been busy exploring the castle.'

'The legend is after being there on the back

of the stone.' Father Flaherty said hesitantly. 'He's put it there to preserve the simplicity of the design.'

'He?'

'Padraic. It is clever hands he has with the stone and the wax.'

As I stepped to the back of the grave marker, a chilling premonition came over me. The legend seemed to leap up at me:

'Countess Saint Brendan O'Leary.' it read. 'Born May 7, 1946. Drowned off the shore of Inish Laoghaire February 20, in the year of our Lord, 1966.'

I stared at it, not quite comprehending at first what it meant. Then, I understood.

Katsy de Gomez had been Bren's wife. I was certain that the new grave contained her body and that she had died very shortly after the newspaper containing my photograph and the story about the debut had arrived on Inish Laoghaire.

'God save me, child! You didn't know!' Father Flaherty's shocked voice came faintly to me.

I leaned against the headstone to support myself; sucking in a deep breath, I was able at last to nod my head.

'Yes,' I said. 'I think I knew.'

The faint scent of flowers crowding about us became suddenly overpowering. The odd sense of calm I had been feeling burst like a child's soap bubble, and I turned and ran blindly from the churchyard.

I wanted suddenly to escape—to leave Inish Laoghaire with its black legend and its festering secrets. I looked out across the seething channel that separated it from the mainland, and thought that I must find Tim Donahue; I would ask him to take me away in his curragh.

I ran and ran, staggering frantically up the steep rise of the island, away from the castle.

*   *   *

I had nearly reached the first outcropping of stone that sprang up on the western slopes of the island, when the lines of the old Count's verse came to me as they had the day that I had looked down into the pit, there inside the walls of the old castle. Just as before, the lines dealing with death were especially emphasized.

The voice seemed to originate somewhere behind me, separating me from Dunleary, and I knew that the sense of danger I felt was very real. A feeling of desperation possessed me, and I plunged down the ridge, remembering again Tim's frank, smiling face and searching almost frantically for some sign of a cottage.

I was halfway down the far side when I saw a small boy—a child of perhaps seven or eight—peering at me from behind a clump of sedge. Even from that distance, there was no mistaking the sharp tilt of his black brows that were pixie-like in that puzzled, young face.

Stunned by the boy's sudden appearance, I stopped. After a moment, he darted away like a startled rabbit and wove his way expertly between clumps of blue gentian and bloody cranesbill. As I watched him go, an overpowering sense of unreality took possession of me. It seemed suddenly that my mind was playing tricks on me, for I imagined that it actually was Bren that I had seen, as he had been as a child when Eileen Maguire had been alive, and the two of them had wandered over the island together. The odd sensation persisted, and for an instant I fancied that I was Eileen, the girl who I suspected had been my mother.

Then I glimpsed the child again. He was peeking at me now from behind a mauve-tinted stone, and I realized that he was no illusion from the past; he was, after all, quite real.

Mrs. Callahan had been right, I thought, and I wondered why Bren had lied to me. Why had he said that there were no children on Inish Laoghaire? Was it because the boy was his son, born of some shameful union with an island woman?

The eerie voice had died away, and some of the panic I had felt left me. I suspected that the child, who had disappeared completely into a jumble of upthrusting stone, was still watching me through some secret niche, and I tried to appear calm, hoping that he might be drawn to me. I wanted very much to talk to him.

There was no sign of a cottage on this far side of the island, and I guessed that Tim Donahue's dwelling must be hidden behind one of the larger outcroppings of limestone. The sudden thought that the boy might be Tim's son came to me and only added to my confusion. For it seemed that if the child did belong to Tim, Bren might, quite simply, have told me.

Beyond the stark rim of the island, the blue sea pulsated with magnificent force; the great, rolling swells galloped in to shatter into shimmering rainbows of spray against the island's stony skeleton. As I drew near the sea cliffs, I became aware of sucking sounds beneath my feet, and knew that there were caves there below the fluted headland.

From this point, I could see the small channel separating Inish Laoghaire from Maguire Island quite clearly, for it was less than a half mile away. It would be a simple matter, I thought, to swim across to Maguire Island at low tide, for it was obviously an extension of Inish Laoghaire just as Bren had said.

I came to a path that followed the brink of the headland and looped about through the upthrustings of stone, coming dangerously near to the edge in places. There were hoof prints showing in the sparse patches of soil, and I knew that Bren must sometimes ride here. The sea, a cauldron of black water and foam, lay far below. At this point, the cliff shelved downward—an unbelievable array of green growth seeming to spring from the very heart of the gray stone.

The dark, seething water seemed to draw me, and, for an instant, I understood Bren's fascination with the sea. I recalled the untrammeled excitement I had first seen in his eyes at Cliff House, when he had gazed out over the vast Pacific.

Shivering a little, I clung to a gaunt pillar of stone that might have been one of the ancient religious relics, so meticulously carved was it by wind and sea. As I leaned against it, gasping, a new sense of foreboding came over me.

Suddenly, I saw the child again; now he clung to an outcropping of stone a few feet down the face of the cliff and gazed up at me, with his odd, soaring brows vivid in his small brown face. I was reminded of Mother's fairies. Was he some strange, beautiful fairy child left by the little people in place of a human child? Was he Bren as a child?

He watched me, his dark head thrown back, oblivious to the writhing sea below. A draft came whipping up off the roaring waves, and he tottered a little, his slight body seeming, for a terrifying instant, to float unattached over the angry water.

I cried out, and heard the thunder of horse's hooves, growing near, coming to me suddenly, as though in answer to my call. I kept my eyes focused on the child as though I could hold him safely with the mere force of my gaze.

The horse came on without a slowing of pace, and a sudden sense of impending disaster caused me to whirl just as the sleek, shining steeplechaser reared over me. I saw the nostrils in the high, proud head flaring and the bright, soft eyes rolled back to show the whites, and I leaped backward losing my grip on the rough stone.

In that final instant, before I fell, I glimpsed dark riding britches, above gleaming, black boots.

'Bren!' My cry was lost in the thunder of the horse's hooves as it raced away.

CHAPTER TWENTY-ONE

I looked up into the sun-browned face of the boy.

'I'm Patrick,' he said, smiling. 'I thought you would fall, like the lady with the black hair. But you caught yourself in time.' His small face grew suddenly somber. 'I shouldn't have liked to see you fall to the bottom, as she did.'

Horrified, I realized what the boy had said. 'You saw her fall?' I asked.

He nodded his head that was as sleek and dark as a young seal's. His eyes became suddenly old and wise in his child's face.

'What a terrible thing for a child to see!' I said, wondering whether or not to believe him.

It occurred to me that someone might have told him of the tragedy, and that he only imagined that he had seen it.

I said: 'You must put it from your mind. Don't think about it anymore.'

He nodded, giving me a little smile.

I lay on a fern-covered ledge, a few feet below the top of the cliff. The mouth of a shallow cave, carved back into the soft, crumbling stone, yawned before me. Bits of limestone lay among the clumps of flowers, and I realized that the boy, Patrick, had been digging there. Gingerly, I raised myself to a sitting position, noticing that there was a bit of blood on one of my hands. Whoever had ridden me down had gone, and I tried not to think that it had been Bren.

'You're hurt,' Patrick said. 'Why did he want to make you fall, too?' he added candidly.

I stared at him. 'You saw who it was on the horse?' I asked.

'I saw his boots,' Patrick said. 'His shiny black boots. Someday I shall have a pair exactly like them, and ride the steeplechasers, as he does. I shan't always wear pampooties.'

I noticed then the odd little skin shoes on his narrow feet, and remembered what Bren had said about making a pair for me. It couldn't have been Bren, I thought. Dear God, don't let it have been Bren!

'There must be others here to wear shiny boots, and ride the horses,' I said. 'Padraic perhaps. Or even Tim.'

'No,' Patrick stated. 'There is only the King. The O'Leary.' He fixed me with his bright, unyielding gaze, which had become as determined as Bren's. 'Who are you?' he demanded then.

'I am The O'Leary's wife,' I said. 'The Countess Saint Brendan O'Leary. You see, darling, it must have been someone else. That, or he simply didn't see me there, beside the stone. Yes, that is it, of course.'

Although the child was no more than seven or eight, it seemed that his gaze became almost pitying.

'The black-haired lady used to come here, too, to this side of the island,' he said. 'With Padraic,' he added, looking wise. 'But it was always the King she was after riding with. Padraic doesn't ride at all. I think he's afraid.'

'You said you saw her fall,' I said.

'He made her fall,' Patrick said. 'I shan't hurt people as he does, when I have my shiny black boots and ride the horses.'

'You shouldn't say a thing like that, unless you are absolutely certain,' I said, with forced

156

calmness. 'Even then . . . I am convinced that the horse coming at me like that was entirely an accident. He didn't see me there because of the pillar.'

'He saw you,' Patrick said, with a bit of stubbornness that reminded me of Bren. 'He saw her, as well. He had on a black hat that day, just like now. It was pulled down very low. But I knew that it was the King, because of the boots.' He paused for an instant, his face pale with the memory, and pointed off down the island. 'It happened just there,' he said. 'Next to the big stone.'

'Bren never wears a hat, darling,' I said, following the line of his pointing finger.

The headland plummeted sharply there, with no ledge to break a fall. I thought: If whoever it was had really wanted to kill me, they would surely have waited until I had wandered farther along the cliff.

'Surely you know that the King never wears a hat,' I continued, feeling much better now that I knew that particular detail.

'Only when he kills,' Patrick insisted.

'It could very easily have been someone trying to disguise himself to look like Bren,' I stated.

Seeing the expression on Patrick's young face, I knew that he was unconvinced, because of the shining boots, which had made a vivid impression on him.

'How old are you?' I asked, overcome with

curiosity about this strange, dark little boy, who looked so remarkably like my husband.

'I'm eight,' Patrick said proudly. 'Old enough to know what dying is.'

'Not everyone is run down by horses and pushed into the sea,' I said.

'My mother is dead,' Patrick said. 'I think she must have died in her bed.'

'When you were very small?'

'I can't remember.'

'And your father?'

'I think he must be dead, too. I live with Tim and Aunt Sheila. We've a cottage just there.' He pointed again, and I saw a twirl of blue smoke rising in a narrow streamer above the island's stony face.

I felt suddenly light-headed. 'Of course,' I said. 'I thought that you might live with Tim.'

A puzzled frown came over Patrick's face at my outburst, and his dark brows beetled, so exactly like Bren's that my sense of discovery vanished at once, giving way once more to doubt.

'Did you tell anyone that you saw the Spanish lady die?' I asked.

'Tim,' Patrick said.

'And what did he say?'

'That my imagination is too keen. That it was an accident that befell her. I wanted to find Padraic, and ask him to tell Tim how it was. But I was afraid. Padraic is cruel.'

'What had Padraic to do with it?'

'He was there. He saw it as well as I.'

You daren't murder me, *brother*—the words that Padraic had said to Bren there on the path above the small harbor, when Bren first brought me to the island, focused suddenly in my mind. Shocked, I stared at Patrick.

'And Padraic didn't try to save her?' I demanded.

'I heard him laughing,' Patrick said. 'I stayed hidden in the rocks, thinking that there would be a donnybrook between the two. Instead, the King got down from his horse, and Padraic slipped his arm about the King's shoulders, as though he were very pleased, and they went away, the two of them together as cozy as could be, leading the steeplechaser behind.'

I felt suddenly ill. 'Did you tell all of this to Tim?'

'Not the part about Padraic and the Spanish woman slipping off together. If Padraic should discover that I had spied on them, he would be angry. You must promise not to tell.'

'You saw them together often, then?'

'They went to the Cave together. The Spanish Cave. It is across the channel, on Maguire Island. Sure I go there myself, to gather eggs from the birds' nests on the cliffs.' Patrick added with pride, 'I have many places on the cliffs where I go to hide. I saw Padraic and the Spanish woman together many times. They were after being together the day the King came riding by on his steeplechaser. The

159

black-haired woman had tied her horse in a patch of gorse, while she and Padraic went rowing off to Maguire Island. The King discovered her horse there. I saw him hide himself and his steeplechaser behind one of the many large stones nearby.'

Patrick pointed once more, indicating a large upthrusting rock. 'Sure he knew the two of them were together there at the Spanish Cave, across the channel. He waited, and when the two of them returned, and the Spanish woman had mounted her horse once more, he dashed out and frightened her steeplechaser, and she fell then.' Patrick looked at me intently, his eyes bright. 'Do you still believe that I have made it all up?'

'I don't know,' I murmured.

'If you believe me, I shall tell you about the Spanish Cave. Sure I might even take you there sometime.'

'The King is my husband,' I protested. 'How can I possibly believe that he is a murderer?'

'Did you let Padraic kiss you?' Patrick demanded suddenly.

I gave him a stunned look.

'If you did, and if you are truly his bride, he will surely kill you. Tim says the King is trying to destroy the legend, and that he will do it in the end. He will find a bride for himself who is true, and who won't be affected by the curse of the Spaniard.'

'A young boy shouldn't concern himself with

such matters,' I reprimanded him.

'I know all about it,' Patrick boasted. 'I know that the old Count's wives died because they were untrue. Sure I heard it down at the village pub. The men there don't know that I'm about.'

Patrick gave a defiant toss of his well-shaped, dark head. Because he looked suddenly very young and lost, and because I myself felt vulnerable and alone, I reached out and pulled him to me.

Patrick's slight body stiffened against me. I thought: I have embarrassed him with my sudden display of affection. Then I saw that he had cocked his head and was listening. The sound of voices came to me, and I realized that someone was above us on the headland.

'Padraic,' Patrick whispered. 'It's together they were after being, he and the King, plotting against you. They've returned to be certain that you fell to your death.'

'Nonsense,' I said, more sharply than I had intended. 'You see, you are imagining terrible things, just as Tim said.'

I started to rise. Patrick tugged frantically at me, pulled me down, crawling back into the shallow cavern and urging me to follow. His brook-brown eyes were suddenly wide with terror.

'Darling,' I said. 'It's only your imagination. Please.'

'I don't want you to die,' he sobbed. 'I want

161

to keep you.' Tears glimmered on his long dark lashes.

I huddled with him in the small cave that was damp and clammy inside, with a crystal pool of water collected in the center of its cupped floor. Sudden love for the child burned in me, perhaps because he was so much like Bren, and therefore so much like my own children would be.

*   *   *

A rock plummeted suddenly past the mouth of the small cave. It tumbled down over the ledges and loosened miniature rivulets of talus that rustled softly downward.

'You see!' Patrick whispered. 'You see, Countess, it is just as I said.'

'Deirdre,' I murmured against his dark head. 'You may call me Deirdre. And the stone falling was no more than an accident. I'm certain of it. There are no more,' I added triumphantly.

Someone above us laughed. Maeve! I was almost joyous, for it wasn't Bren at all up there with Padraic. It was only Maeve, taking a stroll along the cliff.

Was Tim with her, I wondered suddenly, remembering the time I had seen them together. And who had been astride the steeplechaser? The old Count, perhaps? Bridget had told me that he had ridden before his accident. Riding, I thought, was like bicycling or roller skating—one never forgot how.

The murmur of voices grew louder, and I realized that Padraic was there with Maeve. It was impossible to catch the thread of their conversation, and I felt rather foolish, hiding from them. But when I said that we really should show ourselves, Patrick turned pale again, and tugged at my clothes.

'No!' he insisted, his small face desperate.

I realized that his fears were quite real to him, although I had succeeded in convincing myself that a good deal of what he had revealed to me had been no more than some childish hallucination.

It seemed that we crouched there inside the small cave for an eon. After a while, Padraic and Maeve's voices faded, and there was only the sound of the sea and the shrill cries of the gulls coming to us.

'I must go now, darling,' I said. 'I'm sure that it is quite safe.'

'Must you?' Patrick's dark brows arced above his bright eyes, reminding me poignantly of Bren.

'I'll come back,' I promised.

'Tomorrow, Deirdre?'

'Tomorrow,' I said.

*   *   *

Slowly, I made my way to the top of the cliff by clinging to the tough stems of gorse and bracken. My eyes were level with the top, when something white caught my eyes through the screen of green growth. Maeve's spotless robe.

She and Padraic were seated in the shelter of a large stone. Padraic had his arm about Maeve's shoulders. Suddenly, he drew Maeve to him and kissed her. They clung together for a long while, Maeve's white robe straining about the ripe curves of her body.

I hung there, stunned and disillusioned. A moment later, they arose and started up the slope.

I pulled myself up, and because there seemed to be nowhere else to go, I went back to the castle.

*   *   *

I told Bren that night that I had seen Katsy's grave. I spoke very calmly, trying not to sound accusing.

'And you are wondering why I didn't tell you about her,' he said, a hint of fierceness in his voice.

'A little,' I admitted. 'It does seem rather odd. Surely you knew that I would discover . . .what she had been to you.'

'She's dead,' Bren stated. 'I couldn't see that it would make any possible difference. In fact, nothing should, Roisin,' he added, his face stern and compelling me to agree. 'After all, it is you who are my wife now.'

'Not even the child makes a difference, I suppose.' My voice was tinged slightly with sarcasm.

'You are thinking that I lied to you about Patrick,' Bren said. 'I can see it in your eyes.'

'Didn't you?'

'Hardly. If you will remember, we were speaking of the island village when you asked about children. And Dunleary. There are no children here, I assure you.'

'But shouldn't Patrick be here?' I asked. 'At Dunleary?'

I looked up into his brown face, my eyes daring him to deny the thought that was in my mind.

His face grew grim and his devilish brows became more satanic than ever.

'It is better this way,' he said. 'For everyone concerned. And the boy is happy there with Tim. He is in good hands.'

'But . . . I wouldn't mind if . . .' My voice dwindled off painfully beneath the look he flashed me.

'You think Patrick is my son, don't you?' he demanded.

I nodded. 'He's so remarkably like you. What would you expect me to think now that I've seen him?'

'I've not brought you here to go about

forming false conclusions,' Bren said.

'I suppose I am jumping to conclusions to imagine that you all but rode me down today on your steeplechaser,' I said, in an angry voice.

'What in God's name are you blathering about, Deirdre?' Bren demanded, thrusting his dark face near to my own. 'Have you lost your reason entirely?'

I held up my bruised hands, some grievous hurt in me refusing to relent, even though I knew the truth of what he said.

'It was because you rode me down that I fell,' I said. 'Surely you saw me there, beside the stone pillar. Actually, I think it is a cross— one of Saint Brendan's. It saved my life.'

Fear had come into his eyes. He pulled me suddenly against him, squeezing the breath from me and covering my eyes and mouth with hard kisses.

Then he thrust me away.

'Promise me that you shan't go wandering off like that again onto those narrow paths,' he demanded. 'Promise me that you shall obey.' He embraced me again, savagely.

'I am your wife,' I said, with a feeling of dismay.

Later, it occurred to me that he had not denied being there on the far side of the island, astride his steeplechaser.

CHAPTER TWENTY-TWO

The weather on Inish Laoghaire held, and it was sunny and clear again the following day. Bren arose early, donned his handsome, dark jodhpurs and the shining boots, which suddenly seemed frightening, and hurried out to work his steeplechasers. Early morning was the best time for a gallop, he had told me.

My hands smarted a bit as I pulled the blankets up under my chin, and I recalled the frightening incident of the day before. Had it been Bren there on the headland on one of his sleek horses?

Later, when I climbed the stairs to pay my morning call on Mrs. Maguire and saw Bren riding at the far end of the island near the pink bog, his feet high in the stirrups, I felt suddenly reassured.

The frightening tale that Patrick had related to me about Katsy's death had surely been exaggerated, I decided. Father Flaherty had made no mention of horse's hooves having marred the slim, white body in the churchyard. Surely he would have, I reasoned, if it were true that she had been trampled to death before her body was tossed into the sea.

I recalled having had fantasies of my own as a child; I had invented wild little tales simply because I had been so much alone.

I would find Patrick again, I thought, as soon as I had greeted Mrs. Maguire.

Then I remembered my promise to Bren. I contented myself with the thought that it could do no possible harm to go wandering about the island as long as I stayed away from the dangerous paths along the sea cliffs.

*   *   *

The old Count was there in the second-floor corridor when I came back down the stairs.

'Good morning,' I said cautiously as I recalled my torn wedding dress, and the harshly whispered snatches of verse that had come to me from the depths of the castle and from among the scattered stones on the ridge of the island.

'Aye it is,' he said, his bright eyes concentrating on my face. 'Eevelleen,' he added, giving a sad little shake of his head. 'I am bad with names, although I never imagined that anything might cause me to forget yours.'

'Deirdre,' I said, feeling uneasy beneath his luminous gaze.

My eyes strayed to the scar on his temple.

'Eileen Deirdre,' he said, with a triumphant bob of his white head.

'No,' I protested. 'You've turned it about.'

'That last one's name was Katherine,' he whispered suddenly. 'A black, Spanish bitch. She is gone. Did you know that she died?' His

168

eyes had grown crafty.

'Yes,' I said. 'And Eileen, too,' I added, watching his face closely for I knew not what sign.

'Ah no, Roisin. We've only pretended that you were dead. I thought you understood.'

'But why?' I asked, my heart thudding with a sudden, thrilling anticipation.

'Does it matter now? You've come back to us. You've come home to Dunleary.' He leaned close to me, and grasped my arm with a strong, veined hand. 'But you must be careful, Eevelleen. The danger is still here.' His bright eyes commanded me.

'What danger?' I asked, leaning intently toward him.

'Twenty years is a long time,' he said. 'It is no longer clear in my mind.'

His eyes grew vague. His lips trembled.

'Have you another poem for me?' I asked, overcome suddenly with compassion.

'Sure every poem I ever wrote was for you, Eevelleen,' he said, in a soft, sad voice.

'I should like very much to hear all of them,' I said.

We entered his room, where he rummaged through an immense secretary and scattered sheafs of paper as carelessly as a child. Beside the large desk, a row of leather-bound books stood neatly on a shelf. I lifted one down, and opened it to the flyleaf. It was illuminated in the same manner as the book in my mother's

169

rosewood chest.

'Excuse me, please,' I said, an odd sense of calm coming over me. 'I shall be right back.'

Hurrying a little, I went down the long corridor to the large room I shared with Bren, and removed Mother's rosewood chest from the hiding place I had found for it, in one of the immense wardrobes. Fumbling a little, I removed the book of verse, and took it back to the old Count's room.

I untied the pink ribbon, and let it fall open. The cluster of withered flowers went whispering to the floor. The old Count stooped to retrieve them. As he arose, his eyes alighted on the open book, and an incredulous light came into them.

'You've had it all this while,' he said. 'It was you who took it, then?'

'Eileen Maguire was my mother,' I said, very carefully, as though the sound of my voice might in some way disturb the small evidence I had found.

'I illuminated it myself,' the old Count said. He took the book from me, and riffled the crisp pages, an expression of amazement coming onto his face.

'Someone has completed it,' he said.

I saw then that the strange, Gaelic writing on the last pages was different from the bold strokes that filled the front of the book. Finer. Feminine, I thought—like Mother.

'Is that why you came to get it from my

room?' I asked, watching the old Count's face. 'Because you guessed that Mother may have used it for a diary and filled the blank pages with an account of whatever it was that drove her from Dunleary?'

'I couldn't help noticing that you had become a woman,' the old Count mused. I realized that he hadn't heard me—that he was caught up again by Dunleary's inescapable past. 'It seemed strange to me, that you insisted on going off so often with Bren. You were an inspiration, you know. Your devotion to my son was quite obvious, and rather touching. But there was a good deal more to your affection,' he said then, his eyes growing very bright. 'Do you recall the first time I kissed you, Eevelleen? I knew then that you saw more in me than a man grown white with age. Sure it was enough to bring back my youth!'

'You are a handsome man still,' I said, an eerie sense of destiny possessing me.

'Ah, you thought so even then, though I was twice your age!' Suddenly, his eyes clouded. 'But he noticed! Ach, he saw that you were intrigued. And he was determined that I shouldn't have you!'

For an instant, I imagined that he was speaking again of the child, Bren. Then he lowered his voice to a rough whisper.

'The evil one,' he hissed. 'I'd rather see you dead than to give yourself to him. I said it then

171

and I say it now!'

One of his thin hands darted quickly toward me and closed about my arm like a bird's dry talon. Terrified, I pulled free from him and darted from the room.

*   *   *

As I hurried away from the old castle, countless little memories of my mother emerged. She had been in love with the old Count, I thought. Uncle Con had been right about her dubious past. Some dark, unrevealed secret had driven her from Inish Laoghaire, had caused her to change her name, and to lose her true identity forever.

Then, by some mischievous quirk of fate, Bren had discovered my photograph in the *San Francisco Chronicle*, and he had remembered that long lost love of his childhood.

I wished suddenly that I had refused to return with Uncle Con to San Francisco after my parents' funeral. Then, I thought, I should never have become entangled in this tenuous web of doubt and confusion. It occurred to me, as I made my way up the island ridge, that I would never again have peace of mind until the mystery was unraveled. Even as I made my furtive way to the far side of Inish Laoghaire— for I was determined not to disappoint Patrick—an overwhelming sense of evil and disaster went with me.

I had become wary and suspicious of everyone on the island. The old Count. Padraic. Maeve. Even Bren, whom I loved but couldn't quite bring myself to trust.

As I approached the stone crosses where I had stopped to rest the day before, I caught myself listening for the eerie sounds of the illusive voice repeating the old Count's verse. This time, I thought, with a tremulous sense of cunning, I would certainly identify it.

I felt that I was being watched, and turned sharply toward the mainland. I searched for some betraying glimmer, telling myself that it was only Pat Mor, with his glass, that made me feel uneasy.

Even as the thought passed through my mind, the voice came to me again, repeating the verses concerned with death. It seemed to come from beyond the crosses, where gaunt pillars of limestone rose like pale sentinels against banks of wild flowers that were far too frivolous to be growing in this place of evil.

I glanced frantically about, seeking some small movement that might betray whoever had followed me here. Was Bren concealed there behind the stone, on one of his sleek horses? Surely, I thought, there would be some betraying sound, if it were he—the soft flutter of a muffled whinny or the clink of metal against stone. Or it could be the old Count, slipping along in the shelter of the high stone fences, just as I had. Or Padraic. Even Maeve, who I now suspected was not nearly so innocent and pure as she hoped her white robes might indicate.

I took a deep breath, and as I did so, the small rustling sound of air flowing into my lungs drowned out the voice, which had faded gradually until at last it was gone. Had I imagined it after all? Had the many unanswered questions constantly crowding my mind made me slightly hysterical? Was it fear that caused me, from time to time, to desert reason?

Determinedly, I plunged on up the slope, and down the far side of the island. Then suddenly I saw Patrick running toward me. His small face was lighted with a delighted smile which I found so innocently comforting that I felt all strength drain from my knees. I settled down into the fragrant grass to wait for him.

I opened my arms to him, and he came to me, with a shy, glad little laugh.

Had Mother loved Bren like this? Had she felt as lonely and frightened as I did, and found herself also turning to the sweet innocence of a child?

CHAPTER TWENTY-THREE

Patrick had hidden a curragh at the farthest end of the island, where the shallow channel separated Inish Laoghaire from Maguire Island. Just as I had suspected, the islands were not actually separated at all, but clung together beneath the sea. The stony, umbilical cord connecting them protruded from the water in a series of tortuous, limestone loops.

Patrick's young face was eager. 'It's after knowing I was that you would come today,' he said, his brogue becoming more pronounced in his excitement, just as Bren's did. 'And it's after taking you I am to the Spanish Cave,' he added, with a little lilt that I recognized as pure joy.

I hesitated only a moment beside the small, black boat, which was not nearly so large as the one that had brought Bren and me from the mainland to Inish Laoghaire. With Patrick tugging at my hand, I stepped into it, and settled myself, thinking that the channel was hardly dangerous with all of those limestone pillars protruding. Some ridge of stone, still submerged, must have subdued the fierce Atlantic here, making it almost calm.

I tried not to think about Maguire Island and the fact that someday it might belong to me—that perhaps it had been Bren's real

175

reason for seeking me out and marrying me. Instead, I concentrated on Patrick's small, sturdy body pulling the oars.

The gray walls of Maguire Island rose above us. When we had stepped out onto a bit of shingle, at their base, Patrick hid the curragh carefully in a clump of willows growing from a broad fissure. The cliffs here were not nearly so steep as the stark walls that rimmed Inish Laoghaire. But I was aware of the sea always there below us. The path suddenly plummeted and when I cringed back, frightened, Patrick reached confidently for my hand and led me downward.

'Sure it's not as steep as it seems,' he said. 'Even the wee lambs go down.'

A tiny sliver of white beach gleamed below, and an edge of it disappeared beyond an arch of stone, carved by the sea into a frivolous design. Rings of soft green and rose stained the stone, adding an almost tropical, exotic touch to the bit of sand. A stray wisp of sand extended into the black mouth of the Spanish Cave, which lay behind the natural stone portal. From within the Cave came a fearful cacophony of sound.

A line from Milton that Mother had once read to me flickered through my mind: *'Rocks, caves, lakes, fens, bogs, dens and shades of death . . .'*

'It is only the seals,' Patrick said. 'They are after making a fearful noise.'

176

'I don't like it here,' I said, giving an involuntary shudder.

I felt suddenly younger and more vulnerable than this strange, precocious child who reminded me so poignantly of Bren.

'It was there they found her,' Patrick said, pointing. 'The Spanish lady. It was the sea that carried her.'

I saw that the shingle extended well back into the cave. A black channel of water, as wide as a river, rushed back into the darkness, and I wondered where the huge grotto ended. I thought of the moldering skeletons that were said to be lying somewhere in all of that deep, frightening darkness, and I felt an overwhelming urge to get away from that dark, angry place.

Instead, I forced myself to stay and said: 'I hope you didn't see.'

'Aye,' Patrick said, his small face grim. 'I saw. Sure I see everything on these stony islands. And you shall as well, if you become my friend. You shall know all about Tim and Padraic and the rest. And especially about her—the one in white. Sure if you are not afraid,' he added, his face becoming sly. Mischievous, I thought, and even a little cruel—like Bren's.

'It's not polite to spy,' I said sharply. The resentment in my voice was not directed at this child, but at Bren. Who had she been—the woman who had given birth to this charming

177

child? Someone like Katsy de Gomez? One of the fuchsias he had lost his keenness for?

'It would be spying if I went to the castle and peeped in at the windows,' Patrick said. 'But I don't do that. Sometimes, when I am up in the bog or here on the sea cliffs, they come and I see them then. Sure they have no idea that I am near. Eggs wouldn't break beneath my feet, I am that quiet,' he ended proudly, drawing his fine line.

'Padraic and Maeve?' I asked, trying to guess how much the boy knew and understood

'Aye. Maeve and the rest,' Patrick said, avoiding my eyes and suddenly darting back into the huge cave.

I followed him, not quite daring to persist. Who were the rest? Bren? The old Count? What was it that Patrick had seen that made him suddenly avoid me?

Light penetrated the immense sea cave for perhaps a hundred feet. The great, domed roof rose above us, fading into darkness. The walls of the cave were pale, capturing what light there was, and casting it back at us.

A broad ledge of stone, different from the rest—granite, I thought, for it was a shimmering gray color—formed a roadway of sorts above the black channel of water, which surged with the tide, filling the cave with its thunderous roar. I glimpsed movement along the base of the ledge, and guessed that the seals were clustered there.

'The basking sharks don't bother them here,' Patrick said.

'How far back does the cave go?' I asked.

Patrick shrugged his thin shoulders. 'To America, perhaps,' he said.

'The skeletons of the Spaniards,' I said. 'Where are they?'

'You are after seeing them for yourself?'

'No!' I said, repressing a shudder. 'I was only curious.'

'The O'Leary and his men put the Spanish Captain's ship here, as well. They brought it into the cave on the high tide. It is lying there around a crook in the cave, much farther than I can throw a stone.'

'No one is really certain about the ship,' I said. 'Simply because a few gold coins have been found ...'

'Sure I *saw* the ship!' Patrick stated. 'I caught a good many petrels, and used them to light my way into the cave. The ship is after being there, still, lodged against the ledge. The tide was out, and I could have gone into her if I had dared!'

Was the child imagining things again? I stared into his face and fancied that I saw truth in his bright eyes.

'Don't ever do that!' I said, my voice growing sharp again, this time with fear for this strange, lonely child. I gripped his shoulders as though he were my own. 'You must promise me, darling, that you shall never

179

go into the ship.'

'I hadn't enough petrels caught up for the job,' he said, pulling away from me. 'It takes a good many to light the way back to where the galleon lies. And the skeletons,' he added. 'Sure they are propped there against the walls, as though they still live, with no meat left on their naked bones.'

'Tell me about the petrels,' I said, wanting to divert him from the grizzly scene he described. Gently, I urged him about. 'Let's go out into the sun. Perhaps you can point one out to me. I don't know about petrels.'

'They are little black birds,' Patrick said, allowing himself to be led. 'Sea birds, they be. It is after being fond of the oil slicks, they are, and following along in the wake of ships. It's the oil caught up in their feathers that causes them to burn.'

I shivered at the brought of the small, dark birds, flaming like candles.

The sun seemed unbelievably bright outside of the immense cave, which emitted a strong, dank odor. Above us, over the face of the sloping headland, wild flowers bloomed in glorious profusion. Their colors were reflected on the walls of Inish Laoghaire. I thought how beautiful Inish Laoghaire would be, if it were not for the evil hovering over it.

We made our way up from the cave, crawling over the peculiarly shelved landscape. Clouds of small butterflies drifted before us

180

like petals wafted by some errant breeze.

We reached a small glade, nestled halfway down from the top of the cliff, which was composed of ridge upon ridge of worn limestone, with grass and flowers springing from every fissure. A ewe, trailed by a black-faced lamb, grazed nearby and paused now and then to cast a pale, wary eye our way.

'Let's sit here for a moment, and look at the sea,' I said, wishing suddenly that I didn't have to return to Dunleary.

As I slipped down into the grass, my eyes were drawn to a spot of bright blue color. It was one of Padraic's exquisite silk ascots. Something lay beside it, and upon investigating, I found that it was a bulging rucksack.

Patrick told me then that Padraic had visited Maguire Island the previous evening.

'They came together,' he said. 'Padraic and the one in white.'

He turned quickly from me, a flush creeping over his face. I guessed that he had seen them kissing, as I had.

'He must have forgotten this,' I said, curious about the rucksack.

'I know what it contains,' Patrick said.

'You looked into it?'

'There was no need for that, now,' Patrick said. His face became secretive. 'Do you want me to show you what it is?' he added in a conspiring whisper.

181

'It belongs to Padraic,' I said.

'I've something like it of my own,' Patrick said. 'Come.'

He took my arm and led me out of the pocket of green grass onto one of the sheep paths that laced this section of the headland. We entered one of the smaller caves. There were no birds nested here. The bottom of it was clean and smooth.

At the rear of the shallow opening, Patrick removed stones and drew out some sort of a box. He came back to me, dragging it after him across the smooth limestone. I guessed that it must contain his keepsakes, and I tried to imagine what sort of treasures a small boy living on Inish Laoghaire might collect. Birds' eggs, and butterfly wings, and odd bits of fishnet, perhaps?

Very gently, he placed his box before me and looked up expectantly into my face. He wanted very much to surprise me.

'You open it, Deirdre,' he said.

'I hope there are no frogs inside to leap out at me,' I said, lifting the lid.

Patrick's box contained ancient Spanish relics: a number of buttons and small ornaments crafted of metal and crusted and tarnished almost beyond recognition. I glimpsed shoe buckles, inlaid with what appeared to be pearls, and knew at once where Patrick had found them.

'You got them from the skeletons,' I gasped.

'Aye,' he said. 'They were scattered about there in the large cave. Don't you like them, Deirdre?'

I managed a feeble nod, not wanting to disappoint him.

'I can't imagine that Padraic's knapsack is filled with this sort of thing,' I said.

'Padraic takes things from the Spanish ship,' Patrick said.

'But how?'

'Sure he's as clever as a basking shark in the water,' Patrick said.

'And I suppose he uses a petrel to light his way into the galleon,' I said, doubting Patrick again.

'He has an electric torch,' Patrick stated; his small, solemn face looked hurt, I thought, because I had tried to make light of what he had told me.

'Darling.' I pulled him against me. 'I believe you. It's just that I can't understand Padraic. He hardly seems the type to soil his hands.'

'Padraic would do anything for money, Tim says. Padraic would be after choking his own grandmother if it would make him rich.' Patrick flashed me a wise look. 'Gold—isn't it what the whole world wants?'

I knew that this too was something that Tim had said.

'But to risk a life for these piddling bits,' I said. 'A few crusted buttons and the buckles from their shoes—from the shoes of men

183

who—' I broke off, recalling the legend with its dark curse.

'It is more than the buttons he is getting,' Patrick said.

I thought of the treasure Mrs. Callahan had mentioned—the ancient ducats washed up on the Kilmara beach.

'You've seen it—whatever it is that Padraic brings out of the cave in his pack?' I asked.

'No,' Patrick said. 'But I know it is gold. Peek into his knapsack if you would see for yourself.'

'Does Bren know about the ship? The O'Leary. Does he know?'

Patrick shrugged. 'I have never seen him near the cave. Sorra a bit The O'Leary cares for the old tales. It is after killing them off, he is.'

'But if there is gold there . . .' I broke off, thinking that I was becoming as imaginative as Patrick.

I would look into Padraic's knapsack, I decided, going back along the path. Patrick stopped me with a small grubby hand on my arm.

'It is for giving you a wee gift I am,' he said.

He darted back into the small cave and rummaged about. When he returned, I saw something bright clutched in his hand. His eyes glowed with pride as he gave it to me—a small, ornate cross, studded with stones as green and glittering as a cat's eyes.

'It was theirs, too,' I said.

'The best I have found,' Patrick stated.

I thought again of the legend. Had the Spanish Captain, Juan de Medina, brought the cross to Inish Laoghaire as a gift for that long-ago Maeve? I repressed the sudden sense of revulsion that came over me.

'Put it on your chain,' he commanded, pointing at the locket that Bren had purchased for me in Dublin. 'You shan't ever forget me, with the cross dangling about your neck. Not as she did. It's a true friend I want.'

'As who did?' I demanded.

'The Spanish woman. She asked me to bring her here, to the Spanish Cave. I thought she intended to be friends. Ach, it was only the gold she was after. Isn't it what the whole world wants, just as Tim said.'

'And she forgot all about you, after you had shown the cave to her?'

'Sorra bit she cared then, whether I lived or died!' Patrick's voice cracked a little, with bitterness, like a very old man's. 'I wanted her to die,' he added, with a vicious stamp of his foot. 'I'm glad that she is dead!'

Suddenly, I imagined his small alert figure leaping out at the steeplechaser, diverting the animal, and causing it to rear and plunge.

Immediately remorseful that I should find myself capable of entertaining such a thought about a small child, I unfastened the chain and bent down to let Patrick slip the heavy loop of

185

the Spanish cross over the clasp.

The cross dangled heavily between my breasts. It seemed almost to burn into my flesh. For an instant, I felt that I couldn't bear the weight of it there—that it would crush the breath from me. Then I realized how foolish I was being, because of the legend.

'I shall never forget you,' I said, leaning to kiss Patrick's cheek. 'I shall be your friend for always.'

'Do you think that he still wants to kill you?' Patrick asked suddenly, flashing me a worried look. 'He won't you know, if you are true. He is only trying to destroy the legend.'

Perhaps Patrick's words or perhaps the sudden screaming of a flock of gulls nearby caused a sudden chill to come over me. I was certain that we were being watched, and I glanced about, forcing down a feeling of fear, as another flock of birds wheeled above us.

The omnipresence of evil seemed suddenly overpowering, and I began to climb very swiftly up the steep path, aware that Patrick followed close behind.

We passed by the tiny, rock-sheltered glen where Padraic's ascot and the knapsack had been. I noticed, with a start, that they had disappeared.

From the top of the trail, Maguire Island unfolded before us, barren of human habitation. Below us lay the changeable sea: it was green now, with splotches of white foam moving over its rough surface.

I glimpsed something dark bobbing over the narrow channel that separated the two islands and realized that it was a curragh. A dark-clad figure wearing a dark cap pulled low over his forehead was manipulating it with long, sure strokes, and sent it out of sight into a hidden cove.

'It's him!' Patrick said. 'The King!' He flashed me a frightened look. 'He's found out about the gold.'

'No!' I said sharply. 'It was someone else. Padraic!' Then in a gentler voice, 'Come. We've been gone a long while. They will miss me at Dunleary, and Tim and your Aunt Sheila will wonder where you've gotten off to.'

'I'm too old to be fretted over,' Patrick said.

Nevertheless, he followed me down to the clump of willows, where he had concealed the curragh, and pushed the small tarred boat into the water.

Shrieking birds scattered over the sky before us. I guessed that whoever had been in that other curragh was making his way up through the stone arches and pillars to the heights of Inish Laoghaire. I wondered suddenly if he would be waiting there at the top when Patrick and I appeared. The thought set my heart pounding with sudden dread.

We had gained the top of the path, leading upward to the heights of Inish Laoghaire, when I detected a sound coming from beyond the maze of stony outcroppings.

'It *was* him!' Patrick said, behind me. 'Sure it *was* the King.'

The sound repeated itself, the unmistakable ring of metal against stone. Bren's steeple-chasers were well shod against the cruel terrain of the island.

I realized then what the sound had been.

* * *

That night, I heard the voice again, repeating the old Count's verse. The vibrant tones seemed to issue from the very walls.

Bren was with his father, and Bridget had retired to her third-floor room for the night. I was alone in the large chamber I shared with Bren, and I shrunk from the ominous sound, running to fling myself on the mammoth bed.

It seemed to follow me. Frantically, I pulled the heavy hangings closed, to shut it out, and crawled beneath the thick comforters, trying to conjure the sense of private coziness that Bren and I had shared in the big bed.

It occurred to me that Katsy had lain here with Bren, and I found that I had passed beyond the pain that particular knowledge had once aroused in me; I could only lie there shivering with fright.

Who, within the hideous walls of the old castle, was determined to drive me out? Was it the evil one the old Count had alluded to? He had murmured something about a pretense that Eileen Maguire had died. Why? Why had my mother left Inish Laoghaire so mysteriously?

I huddled deep in the mammoth bed praying that Bren would soon return. Was he actually with the old Count? Or had his visit to his father's room been merely an excuse? Was Bren hiding inside the castle's ancient latrine and trying to frighten me?

Inexplicably, the thought made me angry, and I climbed down from the high bed, and went to the door which opened into the unused privy chamber. It stood slightly ajar. I guessed that whoever was trying to frighten me had left it that way purposely so that the sound would come clearly to me.

I took one of the several candles which stood about the room—in the event of a power outage, Bridget had said. I lighted it, and drawing a deep breath for courage, I stepped into the privy room.

The wind blowing in from the cold sea caused a gust of air to come up from the depths of the castle as I held my flickering candle bravely over the empty pit. Its feeble glow was powerless against that thick, oppressive blackness.

Suddenly, I became aware of another presence close by.

'Who is it?' I called. 'I know you are there. Why are you trying to frighten me?'

I caught the sound of breathing—quick, excited little gasps. Too late, I realized that whoever it was had concealed himself in the dark corners behind me. Thrusting the candle before me, I whirled to face that terrifying darkness.

Someone struck my arm and threw me off balance. The candle flew from my hand and struck the stone wall; the taper of light flared briefly before the flame died.

I glimpsed the unmistakable gleam of a well-polished boot as I staggered sideways and attempted to catch myself on the old latrine. Gloved hands, steely inside of their leather trappings, gripped me and forced me against the clammy wall. My head struck the moist stone and something inside of it exploded into a myriad of sparkling fireflies.

Briefly, I fancied that I was a child again, galloping over the fairy mounds in Ohio, in pursuit of the softly lighted little insects.

Then the fireflies were gone and there was only darkness.

I lay over the back of a horse. Feathery fronds brushed my dangling arms and legs. I caught the pungent scent of ferns. I tried to imagine what was happening to me, and was distracted by the throbbing in my head. It subsided momentarily, and I groped for the horse's mane, attempting to right myself. The animal shied, at my touch, and someone walking nearby struck me a sharp blow across the side of my face.

I dangled there stunned, hearing a scream from far off. It sounded vaguely familiar, and for an instant, I imagined that it was myself who had cried out. Then I realized that my mouth was pressed against the rough, acrid coat of the horse, and that it had been someone else.

The sharp cry sounded again—a strident ululation of pain and rage.

It was the last sound I heard before I fainted.

CHAPTER TWENTY-FOUR

I awoke to the shrill sound of my own voice.

'Bren! No! Please, Bren!'

'Roisin! It's all right, now. It's all right.'

A dark shadow loomed over me, and, although the voice was kind, I shrunk away.

'Bren!' I uttered a terrified little cry, as a strong hand closed over my own.

'No, mavourneen, it is not Bren. It is only me. Tim. Tim Donahue.' I opened my eyes wide, and saw him leaning over me. He added, in a soft voice, 'So you were coming to me, Roisin.'

I tried to remember how I came to be with Tim, and couldn't. I moved my head from side to side, and was rewarded with a burst of pain.

'I'll watch over her, while you go to fetch him,' a woman's voice said. 'Sure he must be out of his mind now, wondering where she has gone.'

Tim disappeared, and I looked up into the face of a woman who looked a good deal like the old Count.

'It is her daughter, you would be,' she said, in a soft, amazed voice. 'The daughter of Eileen Maguire.'

I tried to nod. The slight movement jarred something excruciating inside my head. I must have paled, for the woman said: 'My Lord and Savior, it is a beastly fall you've had.'

'Who are you?' I asked.

'I am Sheila. Sheila O'Leary, sister to the old Count. Rest now, dearie, Tim will soon be back with himself.'

'Himself?' I said, the sound hardly more than a rustle of air between my dry lips.

'Your husband, dearie. The King. Who else?'

I tried to protest. Sheila O'Leary silenced me with a finger to my dry lips.

I lay quietly, trying to recall what had happened. The voice, I thought, and then I had gone into the spooky old privy chamber. And *he* had been there, waiting . . .

I began to sob. Sheila O'Leary was beside me in an instant, placing a cool hand on my forehead.

'Ah, now, darlin', sure it's not as bad as all of

that. Tim will fetch Dr. Riordan from the mainland and be back with him in a short time. It's a marvel with a curragh, Tim Donahue is, even though he is after being my own son.'

'But you said your name was O'Leary,' I said, in a dazed voice.

'O'Leary it is. Tim is a love child, dearie. Never a finer son blessed his face.' She stood over me, placing her hands on her ample hips. Her eyes, which were the same shade as Bren's and the old Count's, shone honestly in her plain face. 'I've shocked you on top of the rest, I can see it in your eyes. You've not heard of my sinning, then? This is the first?'

'No one told me,' I said.

'I was that keen for Donahue,' Sheila O'Leary mused. 'I wouldn't have wanted it to be any different for myself than it has been. Sure he was a fine man, and after making an honest match, when I told him there was to be a child.'

'What happened?' The pain in my head had subsided a little, and I raised myself on one elbow to look at this still handsome woman. She was Bren's aunt, and I thought, perhaps irrelevantly, that she might be able to help me.

'God save me, it was a long while ago,' she said. 'Donahue died a short time later. A fisherman, he was, going out after mackerel in his own small craft. It was the sea that claimed him. He hadn't the strength left to put up a decent fight. Sure she drained it all from him, a man of conscience like himself.'

'There was some other woman, then?'

Sheila O'Leary nodded. 'The one in white,' she said.

Maeve. I wanted to ask how it had been, but Tim reappeared then, and I saw with a deep breath of relief that he was alone.

'Where is Bren?' I asked, breathing my husband's name tremulously.

'Gone after Dr. Riordan, though there is nothing left to be done, but to sign the papers of death,' Tim said.

I stared at them both, suddenly paralyzed.

'But I didn't die,' I whispered. 'I am still alive.'

'You didn't know that Mrs. Maguire was found dead in her bed?' he asked. 'God save me, Roisin, I thought you knew—that it was sorrow that had sent you wandering among the crofts to find me. Or fear, perhaps . . .'

'I had no idea that my grandmother had died,' I said. 'You see, I didn't come searching for you. Someone accosted me inside the castle. Knocked me senseless. I'm certain that it   was . . . was Bren. I saw big boots. He must have brought me to wherever it was that you found me.'

'Lying at the base of the path, which leads down to the channel between the islands,' Tim said. 'Though you must be mistaken about Bren. Sure he wouldn't harm a hair on your

194

head, Roisin, he is after being that fond of you.'

'And you yourself had business there on that dark path, as late as it was?' Sheila O'Leary flashed her son a suspicious look.

I turned away from the two, sensing some area of distress between them.

'First and last, I am a man,' Tim said in a low voice.

'How did she die?' I asked of Mrs. Maguire, turning to look once more at Tim, who stood above me grim-faced.

'According to Mrs. Kelly, the poor woman smothered in her bedclothes, God give her rest.'

'It was an accident, then?' I thought of the old Count's wives and Katsy de Gomez.

'The curse,' Sheila said, before Tim could reply. 'Sure it was the curse at work again.'

'Mrs. Kelly stepped out for a few minutes, and when she returned, Mrs. Maguire had been carried off,' Tim said.

'She should never have crossed the channel that separates the two islands,' Sheila O'Leary said. 'Passion undoes a woman. Makes her foolish.'

'But it was Eileen who loved the old Count,' I said. 'Eileen Maguire. I know now that she was my mother.'

Sheila nodded.

'Sure the old Count was a fine-looking man, then,' she said. 'And Eileen's mother—your grandmother, dearie, widow that she was—had become keen for one of the village men. Pat Mor, it was, he who lives now on the mainland, at Kilmara. It was all arranged for them with the priest, when he fell from his boat and lost his legs.'

'Pat Mor who has the glass?'

'The same. It affected him for a time. He refused to let her see him, though they say that it was his only wish, as he lay mending in his sister's cottage at Kilmara, to watch the island through his glass. It was the glass that kept him alive then, and it is the glass that has afforded his only pleasure since. It is not an accident that Mrs. Maguire's bed stands in a window overlooking the wild sea, and the mainland beyond, although those who know Pat Mor have long since forgotten his real reason for watching the island. It has become a pleasant pastime, for those who know him there in Kilmara, to listen to his stories.'

'Ran away, he did,' Tim said. 'And has regretted it since the day your grandmother had her stroke. Then, God save them both, it was too late.'

'And—my mother. Eileen Maguire. Did she run away?' I asked.

'If her own daughter doesn't know, who can say?'

'She never spoke of Maguire Island or Inish Laoghaire,' I said. 'Whatever her reason for going, it was something she could never bring herself to discuss.'

'It was in a terrible hurry she left,' Sheila said. 'I can see her now, her pale hair whipping about her face, which was half-wild with grief. Clutched a small, drenched bouquet, she did; the little white bog flowers, and a packet of some sort caught up against her breast, as though it meant a good deal to her. It was wrapped in a scrap of oilskin, and a blessing, too, for her clothes were that wet, as though she had fallen into the sea. I tried to question her, while I hung them to dry before the burning turf. But she was that upset that she couldn't reply. Her eyes now, they were red with crying, and her body trembled so that I feared it would break in half. It was after Tim, she was, to row her across to the mainland. She was after seeing Dr. Riordan, she said. I am no saint, understand, and I was influenced by the curse. I knew my brother, the old Count. He had always been keen for the girls, and the two of them in love . . .' Sheila paused, to give me a sad smile.

'I hadn't the heart to question the poor thing in front of Tim, who was only fourteen at the time, though he was as strong as any man and that clever with a curragh.' Sheila gave a little shrug. 'It was only natural that I should have thought the girl had got John's child, and what else could we have done under the circumstances? I had no idea but that she would return with Tim that same day, and the pair of them go to Father Flaherty to right their sin.'

'My mother was a good woman,' I said.

'Ah, and she was,' Sheila said. 'Running off to America, escaping the curse and its dire consequences. I have no doubt that she would have died here, like the others, if she had stayed. She begged me not to tell a soul, that day, that she had come to us. In spite of my promise, I saw to it that Mrs. Maguire knew once I understood that Eileen had left the island for good. Though the poor woman seemed not at all surprised to hear that her daughter had disappeared. The words were gone from her mouth, by then. But I saw by the eyes that she knew, and why.'

'Mrs. Kelly told me that my mother was good,' I said. 'A virgin—'

'I realized later that I was mistaken about Eileen's reasons for going,' Sheila said. 'Though at the time, it seemed only reasonable to assume that she had been caught.'

'The curse,' I murmured. 'It has affected you all, just as Mrs. Callahan said.'

*   *   *

The pain in my head had dwindled to a dull throb. I insisted on sitting up on the low cot, and saw that I was in the main room of a cottage very similar to the cottage at Kilmara where Bren and I had taken tea, with Tim,

198

before setting out for Inish Laoghaire.

The cot beneath me was spotless. I wondered if it was Patrick's, and asked about the child.

'I've given him a wee corner of my own bed,' Tim said.

'He's a delightful child,' I remarked.

'Sure and you are wondering whose he is,' Tim said.

I confessed that I was.

'A sprite, perhaps,' Sheila told me.

I didn't miss the quick glance she flashed at Tim—one of questioning and doubt, I thought.

'We found him on the doorstep,' Tim said. 'A wee, wet mite, screaming his heart out.'

'The cord on him was fresh cut,' Sheila said.

'There is no mistaking the brows,' I said. 'They are exactly like Bren's.'

'Or the old Count's,' Sheila said, flashing me a startled look.

After a while Tim left to go down to the harbor. He would fetch the good doctor, he said, and tell Bren where I was when the two of them arrived.

I started to protest, then thought better of it.

'Patrick is obviously an O'Leary,' I commented, after Tim had gone.

'Obviously,' Sheila O'Leary agreed. 'There is no escaping the curse on this island. There is no virtue left. It has affected us all. Belief in it has become the great besetting sin.'

'But why should it affect you so?' I demanded, surprised to discover that I had grown almost defensively angry.

'People have a habit of doing that which is expected of them. Sure I expect Tim to go out into the sea and bring home fish, just as his father did before him. He does that.'

'And everyone expects me to have some sort of sordid affair and then to die a tragic death, because numerous O'Leary wives before me have become wantons and died,' I said.

'Ach, yes, dearie. And you yourself are afraid that you will do that which is expected of you here on this dreary island. Just as I myself did. Oh yes, my father, who was Count before my brother and the young King, expected me to disgrace him by carrying on with the fishermen from the village. Just as John expected his wives to betray him, and of course they did. At least, that is the story among the men in the village.'

'They died for their sins,' I murmured.

'You believe that it was God who destroyed them?'

'I don't know,' I said.

Sheila O'Leary lowered her voice.

'My Lord and Savior, it wasn't Him up there who struck them down. The lot of them were murdered, take it from me who knows.'

I felt no surprise at her strange revelation—only a kind of full-blown sense of relief welling up in me. It seemed that I had known it all the

200

while and that knowing had been a part of the evil.

'And Katsy?' I said. 'Bren's first wife.'

'Murdered, dearie, as sure as I am standing here before you. It happens only to them—the wives of the O'Leary men—as though their seed must be forever denied.'

'The curse again,' I said. 'Revenge from the grave for all of those half-Spanish infants who were tossed into the sea by that long-ago O'Leary. But somehow O'Learys have managed to survive.'

'And a struggle it has been to do it,' Sheila said. 'Take Bren, for instance. We nearly lost him several times as a wee child.'

'Accidents?' I asked.

'He had his share of falls and scraped knees, the same as Patrick. Dunleary is an eerie place, full of dangerous nooks and crannies to tempt a child, although Mrs. Maguire and Eileen guarded him well enough. One of them was always about when the old Count began to suspect that there was evil afoot.'

'But all of these years . . .' I said. 'If there is someone here on the island who is a murderer . . .'

'Sure no one has yet been able to pin it down, though they go about there at Dunleary looking askance at one another.'

'Whoever it is is terribly clever,' I said. 'A little mad.' I thought at once of the old Count. 'Padraic told me that madness runs in the family,' I added.

'Nonsense, dearie,' Sheila O'Leary snapped. 'Perhaps Padraic himself is the one, although he has his excuses. Even when she died—the Spanish girl—he claimed not to have been there on the headland. He said that it was Tim who had been seen there cavorting with her.'

'Aye,' she added when I could only stare at her.

'But she was Bren's wife,' I said.

'And cozying up to every other man on the island, with my Tim no better than the rest. He was taken in, as they were, God save him.'

'And Bren? Did he know?'

'He knew, but not before he had taken her to the altar. He is after being a man with scruples, and her after him from the beginning.'

'But I thought she came here after Padraic,' I said. 'He had purchased some antiques from her mother.'

'She had no eye for Padraic after she arrived here and found that Bren was king of all of this.' Sheila made a broad gesture intended to indicate the length and breadth of the island. 'And more,' she added. 'O'Learys have wealth, a fact which Padraic resents. He had hoped to succeed my brother as Count and to gain control. However, my brother chose Bren, who is naturally frugal, with a head for business.'

'So Padraic seduced Bren's bride,' I said.

'It was no difficult task, I'm thinking,' Sheila

O'Leary said. 'There are no young women left on the island, though there are a good many Irishmen in their prime, and not without their share of good looks. They have their ways to fudge the virtues of a woman, and a woman lets it be known the sort of treatment she expects from the men she meets. The Spanish girl was no exception. She asked a good many questions about the island, according to Tim, who, God save him, knows well enough the kind of woman she was.'

Sheila O'Leary busied herself at the tall dresser, and a silence fell between us. I lay back on the cot contemplating what she had revealed to me, and the unexpected death of Mrs. Maguire, who had been my grandmother. A gush of hot tears filled my eyes, but I felt certain that the stricken woman had known who I was, and I took comfort in the thought.

*   *   *

I dozed and, when I awoke, Tim still had not returned.

'It's the mist,' Sheila said. 'It has risen, as thick as the fleece off a sheep. The King is accustomed to it, however,' she added quickly. 'He needs no compass to find his way back to Inish Laoghaire. They should be arriving here any minute. Now, dearie, how is it you are feeling after your little nap?'

'Better,' I said. I sat up on the cot.

Surprisingly, a good deal of the pain had gone, and there was only a dull ache at the back of my head.

'Ach, darlin'. I'm glad to hear that.'

The wind sounded vicious outside.

'I can't imagine a curragh out in all of that,' I said.

What if Bren doesn't return, I thought. What if the sea takes him? A shocking sense of loss came over me.

'He'll be back, and soon.' Sheila O'Leary laid a comforting hand on mine. 'It is after being his kind of night with the salt spray flying about. There is nothing to fear. Sure he's a man and an O'Leary who would draw the devil himself in the wake of a curragh.'

A moment later, Patrick poked his head into the main room of the cottage.

'Deirdre!' he said, coming to me; his slim, unmistakably masculine body was enveloped in a long flannel nightshirt. 'It is you, I was thinking, when I heard the voice. Did you come to see me?'

'Now there is a man for you,' Sheila O'Leary said, in a fond voice.

'I . . . I fell down the path, and Tim found me,' I said to Patrick. 'I'm feeling better now, and I really should get back to the castle. Mrs. Maguire has died.'

Sheila gave me a disapproving look.

'She was my grandmother,' I said. 'It's the least I can do. See that she's decently prepared. Stay with her.'

'It's the devil's own night,' Sheila said. 'Not a time for a woman to be venturing out alone.'

'I'll take you back to Dunleary,' Patrick said. 'Sure I've eyes like a cat, and I've my new torch, which Tim gave to me.'

'And when they come, Tim and the King, bringing the doctor?' Sheila asked.

'There's a good chance that we'll meet them on the path,' I said.

CHAPTER TWENTY-FIVE

It was even darker than I had imagined. The mist hung about us like a soft, wet blanket, absorbing the beam from Patrick's flashlight. The mist seemed to have smothered the wind.

The pain in my head increased. It was important to me to get back to the castle, and I tried to ignore the persistent throbbing over my temple.

I tried to remember exactly what had happened. Vaguely, I recalled bobbing along on the back of a horse. Had it been one of Bren's steeplechasers? I had glimpsed a shiny boot in the privy chamber before the fireflies began to dance through my head. There had been no mistaking it. Bren was the only person who wore riding boots on Inish Laoghaire, I thought. Unless . . . The old Count had once ridden, and no doubt had his riding clothes still stored there in the castle. It seemed quite possible that he might own boots I had never seen.

Then as suddenly as it had come, the thought was dismissed, for whoever had accosted me had been strong—strong enough to carry me from the castle to a waiting horse.

Suddenly, I recalled the scream I had heard, as I hung helpless across the back of the sleek animal. Had it been the cry of a gull? Had I only imagined that it had been human? I concentrated in an effort to remember it clearly as I stumbled along behind Patrick through the mist, following the soft round splotch of light cast by his torch.

Patrick seemed totally at ease in the thick, wet darkness, and, needing suddenly to hear the sound of a voice, I praised his ability to find his way. He told me that he often explored the island on a black night. It was the best time, he said, to steal baby rabbits from a warren. Although I thought what a strange little waif he was, I felt grateful for his precocious competence, for I sensed more strongly than ever the evil all about us.

The lights of Dunleary—little halos of brightness glowing faintly through the mist—appeared suddenly below us and I realized that we had gained the top of the island ridge. The sound of the sea was muffled here, and I fancied that I heard some strange sound ahead of us. It sounded like a moan, softened by the mist.

Then I caught the unmistakable clatter of metal against stone, and the fluttery blowing of a horse. An icy chill came over me. I clutched Patrick, pulled him down behind a dark, looming stone, and reached quickly to snap off his torch.

'Sure it is only a steeplechaser,' he said, in a disgusted voice. 'One of the King's.'

'No, darling!' I whispered. 'No! I heard someone. Someone is there ahead of us on the path.'

'Padraic?' A voice cried out. 'Is that you? For the love of God, hurry!'

I realized that it was Maeve.

'Something has happened to her,' I said, springing up, hurrying down the slope toward the sound of her voice.

'Maeve! It's me! Deirdre!' I cried.

Patrick flashed his light and the beam picked up the white of her robe. She sat leaning back against one of the tall stone fences, her robe flowing out from her stately figure. A blanket had been bundled behind her to protect her back from the harsh stones.

'Maeve!' I cried. 'Whatever are you doing here? Are you all right?'

I leaned over her, the cross Patrick had given me dangling down before my face. The light from Patrick's torch caught it and struck bits of fire from the brilliant stones.

'You!' Maeve hissed, her face twisted suddenly with malice. Her hand darted out and tore the cross from my neck. 'You had no right to wear it! No right at all,' she snarled. 'He brought it for me, do you understand? For me! Maeve!'

I remembered the time that I had seen Padraic kissing her there above the headland. Did she think Padraic had given the cross to me?

'It belongs to Patrick,' I said, drawing away from her furious gaze. 'He found it.'

'No!' Maeve cried. '*He* brought it from Spain! My lover left it here for me, and all of the rest of the pretty things hidden in the cave.' She threw back her head and her hair whipped loose about her face. 'He's coming back, do you hear?' She flung the shrill words at me. 'He's coming back to marry me. I am to be his bride.'

'Padraic?' I asked. 'Padraic is coming?'

'Padraic!' She spat the name. 'It is the Captain Juan de Medina I am speaking of. My true love, dearie! My true love! And he shall find me here waiting, dressed in bridal white.'

'But hardly pure, dear Aunt.' Padraic materialized out of the darkness.

'She's mad!' I said. 'Maeve is mad!' I repeated, as though in a dream.

'Quite right, dear sister,' Padraic said, slipping his arm around my shoulders. 'You understand that I must take Deirdre back to the castle, don't you, Aunt?' He glanced at Maeve. 'And then I shall return to you, and escort you safely from this stony ridge.'

'No! I shan't let you take Deirdre!' Patrick thrust himself suddenly against Padraic's tall unyielding form. 'I shan't let you!'

'But you shall be coming too, my valiant little jackeen,' Padraic said. 'I shouldn't think of not including you in my impromptu little party.'

'The child stays,' Maeve said, sounding quite normal again. 'I shall keep Patrick here with me until you return.'

'Ah, the doting mother,' Padraic scoffed. 'How touching, after all of these years of ignoring the child's existence. Really, Aunt, are you certain that it's wise? What if he should go running off through the darkness to that dolt, Tim?'

'He stays with me,' Maeve insisted. 'I won't allow you to take him.'

'I'm certain that your beloved Captain de Medina will approve the boy's presence,' Padraic said, 'when he comes sailing in from Spain.'

Maeve's face twisted into its former expression of ugliness and malice.

'You won't tell him about the child!' she screamed. 'I will kill you if you do! Do you understand me? I will kill you!'

'Of course, dear Aunt,' Padraic said, in his remote, cynical voice. 'However, even you

209

must realize that the secret of his existence can't be kept if he is permitted to run free like a wild lamb.' He reached out a long arm, and drew Patrick away from her. 'It is time you visited Dunleary,' he said to the boy. 'Any fool can see that it is where you belong.'

Patrick suddenly tugged against him and stumbled backward, tripping over Maeve's legs.

Maeve emitted a sharp cry of pain. It was the same sound that I had heard earlier, while I dangled in a fog of pain across the back of the horse. Maeve clutched at her ankle: her face was white in the glow from Patrick's torch.

'God save me,' she gasped. 'I've given it a bloody twist on the stones.'

'My beloved brother will soon be arriving, with Dr. Riordan,' Padraic said in a disinterested voice.

Patrick continued to twist beneath Padraic's arm, which held him like a steel band. Briefly, Padraic released his hold on me and gave Patrick a sharp blow across the side of his head.

'No!' I cried. 'He's only a little child!'

'And as savage as any O'Leary,' Padraic said. 'It's time that wild black strain was subdued.'

I considered Padraic's strange remarks to Maeve. Was Maeve Patrick's mother? It occurred to me that Padraic was Irish for Patrick. Was Padraic, then, the father of this beautiful child, who so closely resembled

210

Bren?

'If he were your child, that would prove that you are an O'Leary after all,' I said.

'You've a keen imagination, Deirdre,' Padraic said, pulling me after him down the island ridge. 'However much I hate to disappoint you, I must inform you that this little bastard is no seed of mine.'

'Whose, then?' I asked.

'Can't you guess, my dear?' Padraic said, with an insinuating laugh.

*   *   *

We entered the castle courtyard. The mist here was scented by Padraic's many flowers. It clung to my skin and hair like perfume. Padraic, with Patrick limp now beneath his arm, led me into the castle and toward a door at the far end of the great hall, which, Bren had once told me, led downward into the vaporous depths of Dunleary. The castle dungeon, Bren had called it.

Now, as Padraic stood back from the yawning door, urging me to enter, I pulled back from him with a sharp protest.

'Come, now, darling,' he said, in an amused voice. 'Surely you don't suspect *me* of being a Blackbeard.'

'Where are you taking us?' I demanded. 'Why?'

'To my own private quarters,' Padraic said.

211

'You must understand that it is for your own safety. You must know by now that someone inside this gloomy castle is trying to do you harm.'

I flashed him a disbelieving look, not quite trusting him.

'You know who it is?' I asked.

'Certainly, darling,' Padraic said. 'Why do you suppose I am trying to help you now?'

Hesitantly, I looked up at him; the pain reeling through my brain confused me.

'Who?' I whispered.

'Would you believe me if I told you?' Padraic asked, his lips twisting into a skeptical smile.

He reached to flick on a light and led me down a steep, mossy stair. I followed numbly, and as we penetrated the moldering gloom I glimpsed great boxes of worm-eaten wood. Tuns and casks of all sizes were piled into half-open rooms that opened off a cavernous corridor; they were tumbled carelessly in their layers of dust, like a child's neglected blocks.

Padraic drew me to the farthest end of that horrible black place, where he paused to unlock an intricately carved, highly polished door. It opened to reveal a room that was astonishingly unreal, for it was as vividly sensuous as the tall rosy-haired man who smiled down at me, waiting for me to enter.

Padraic's blue eyes had become as brilliant as chipped glass; his red head glowed against

212

the unexpected opulence of rich tapestries and oriental rugs.

'My private domain,' he said. 'You see, darling, it isn't nearly so dreadful in the bowels of this old castle as Bren has led you to believe.'

He released Patrick, who stood looking dazed, and turned to secure the door with an immense iron lock.

Suddenly, the evil was all about us.

'I can't imagine why you've brought us here,' I gasped. 'Bren will be returning soon. And Tim. They shall be looking for us.'

'What a shame that they shan't be able to find you,' Padraic said. 'And all to your own good, of course.'

'It's not Bren who wants to harm me,' I cried. 'It's not Bren. He loves me. He wouldn't . . .'

'Deirdre!' Patrick's frightened cry silenced me.

I slipped my arm around the child, drawing him against me.

'It's all right, darling,' I said. 'Tim will come. He'll find us.'

'And your precious husband, the young Count? King Leary?' Padraic asked, with a knowing smile. 'Perhaps I have convinced you at last that he is mad, like the old Count.'

My face burned under the knowing look he gave me.

'And Bren,' I stated. 'He will help Tim. They

will come.'

'What is Padraic going to do to us?' Patrick demanded.

'Reveal to you my most priceless treasures, jackeen,' Padraic said. 'You shall see that you are not the only one to have discovered the Spaniard's rich hoard. Dear Maeve. She has some insane idea that it all belongs to her. But I am the one responsible for finding it in the first place. Who else would have thought of traveling to Spain to bargain for the De Medina artifacts?'

'I fail to see the connection,' I said.

'They kept remarkably accurate records in those days, dear Sister,' Padraic flung wide another door and beckoned me toward it with a slim, sensuous hand. 'You see, darling, I purchased all of the De Medina manuscripts from the Countess de Gomez. The old parchments revealed to me exactly what cargo the ill-fated Captain Juan de Media carried aboard his galleon when he journeyed northward, that second time, bringing bounty for his bride. It seems that he had intended to impress the regal O'Leary with his monstrous wealth. There were any number of chests aboard De Medina's galleon, brimming with gold and precious stones. The little cross Patrick found, and presented to you . . . I recognized it instantly when we were all seated at dinner this evening, darling. You were careless to let it slip from its warm hiding place.' Padraic gave me a wicked leer and glanced at Patrick, who stood white-faced beside me.

'You see, my little jackeen, I have known all along that you were spying on me. What a disgusting annoyance it has been at times.'

I held back, refusing to peer into this second chamber of Padraic's lair, and he reached suddenly for me and drew me roughly across the thickly carpeted floor.

Patrick followed, whimpering a little.

There were people grouped inside the second room. I emitted a startled cry. Then I realized that they weren't real for Bren had told me that Padraic worked in wax. I became aware of the setting in which the wax figures were placed and uttered another startled cry when I glimpsed a skeleton chained to one wall and a great metal animal standing nearby. A door in its broad side stood open, revealing the contorted form of a man inside. Beneath it, an artificial fire glowed.

'Katsy de Gomez bronze bull,' I said, in a disbelieving voice.

I realized that the tortured form inside resembled Bren.

There were other familiar figures in the room: the old Count. Catherine. No! Katsy de Gomez. Katsy de Gomez O'Leary, after whom Catherine had patterned herself. And myself! The glass eyes of the wax figures seemed to follow me.

I turned quickly away, horrified.

'It's not really you, Deirdre,' Padraic said of the form that so closely resembled myself. 'Surely you've guessed by now that she was your mother. Dear little Eileen. Eileen Maguire. And now,' he added, with a wicked chuckle. 'I fully intend to add you to my motley collection.' His voice had become unmistakably suggestive. A lurid shadow seemed to hover beneath the surface of his blue eyes.

'They are horrid,' I said. 'Not at all like real people. And you! You are quite horrid, too. To have created this . . . this atrocity.'

'You disapprove of my wax museum and torture chamber, I assume,' Padraic said. 'Really, darling, think what a remarkable tourist attraction this could be. The steamer would operate between our small harbor and the mainland to convey the bloody fools out here. Naturally, I would emphasize the legend, replete with a modern-day Maeve. Perhaps the Spanish Cave might be opened once I've retrieved its rare wealth. Of course, that shall take some time. And all of my wild talk of tourists is, after all, only a cover-up.' Padraic gave me a coldly amused look. 'It is quite possible that the gold hidden in the cave, in the bowels of that stinking old hulk will last me for the remainder of my natural life. Although my tastes are quite lavish, my dear. Actually, I've not been as free as I would like to indulge

216

them. However, once the islands belong to me
. . .' He gave a little shrug, his voice trailing off.

'I shan't be compelled to slip off on my little
journeys, then,' he continued. 'Carrying furtive
bits of gold hidden carefully about my person
and in my luggage. I shall go forth quite boldly,
flaunting my wealth. I shall be sought after as
the fabulous Count O'Leary, my dear. You
see, that is something else I intend to lay claim
to—my rightful title as the eldest son and my
place in international society. I shall be King
then. The O'Leary. And I shall play the role to
the hilt. Bren has never fully appreciated his
rank in this world. He might just as well be a
pleb for all it has meant to him.' Padraic's face
hardened and became masklike in its smooth-
skinned perfection. 'Do you think that I intend
to live my life out here as he has done?
Existing on the miserable stipend he awards to
me each month? My dear brother's miserable
charity is hardly fit to support a pauper!'

I felt weak with horror. So it was Padraic,
after all, who was the evil in this castle and had
lured me into this hateful dungeon, filled with
his hideous collection. I must escape with
Patrick. Somehow, I must save us both.

'You seem to have done very well on that
stipend,' I said, as calmly as possible. 'The
Condesa de Gomez was a friend of my
cousin's. I know that you paid a good price for
these . . . these instruments.'

'And you haven't done them justice, darling,'

217

Padraic said, becoming suddenly gentle. He tilted my face with his moist hand. 'Why, you are actually trembling. And your lips are quite pale. You see, dear, I stripped the skeletons of the dead Spaniards, moldering in their green slime, and carried the bits of treasure painstakingly to various museums on the continent, where not too many questions were asked as to their origin. There were also bits of the larger treasure in the old galleon that had worked free. I carried them off to Spain, where they love gold. Ah, and there have been women in my life, darling. Eager dowagers, met on my rare little holidays, who have been lavish with their purses when it came to, ah, repaying certain favors which I quite willingly bestowed upon them—for a price, of course. I am an attractive man. You know that as well as they. I've seen it in your eyes.' He turned to indicate the torture room, with a sweep of his long arm. 'I have managed to scrounge enough money, one way or another, to permit me this rather extravagant purchase. Your dear husband, the young Count! King! The fabled O'Leary! considered it all a bit of junk. Boor that he is, he hadn't the least idea of its worth. He assumed that I purchased it all for mere farthings. He has no idea how my chambers here beneath Dunleary are decorated. Not that I've regretted being able to move about as I please.'

'You intend to kill Bren,' I said. 'You intend

218

to kill us all. It has been you, all along, causing those dreadful accidents that happened to the old Count's wives . . . to Katsy, and myself. Even poor Maeve, lying out there in the cold. I suppose you pushed her.'

'No, darling,' Padraic said, in a patient voice. 'Murder is hardly my forte.'

'Then who?'

'Don't you know?' Padraic leaned very near to me, holding me with his icy eyes. 'Surely you must have guessed. The steeplechasers. The shiny boots.'

'Bren?' I said, in a child's disbelieving voice. I had become so certain that it was Padraic. The evil seemed to be there all about us, closing in. 'But of course Bren wasn't even born when the first of the old Count's wives died. Your mother. She fell down the stairs. You must have been a monstrous child, to push your own mother . . .' My voice had risen, and I thought, with some still-sane part of my mind, that I was growing hysterical.

Patrick crowded close to me, his small hands groping, and his presence calmed me. I must save us both, I thought again.

'You have managed to learn a good deal since you came here,' Padraic said. 'An intelligent girl such as yourself must have realized, then, that the old Count is quite insane. I have come to believe that madness is part of the curse. My dear mother, married to a man like that. What chance did she have?'

'It was a fall that made the old Count as he is,' I stated. 'He couldn't have been . . . as he is, when your mother died!' My voice lacked conviction. 'I'm not afraid of him,' I added, defiantly. 'I'm not afraid.'

'Not even of rearing horses?' Padraic asked.

'You saw?' I gasped.

'From a distance. Maeve and I had gone for a walk. We saw you fall, darling. But when we came to the edge of the cliff, you were gone.'

'She was in my cave, with me,' Patrick said. 'I saved her from him. I saved her from the King. Sure I thought you and he were both after killing her.'

'Ah, no, my little jackeen,' Padraic said softly. 'Harm Deirdre? Never in a thousand years.' Padraic paused to flash me a triumphant look. 'There you are,' he gloated. 'They are both mad. Bren and the old Count. I've suspected it for some time. The voice . . . surely you've heard it, Deirdre—whispering eerily of death, quoting bits of poetry that seemed suited to the mood of the victim. And there is the matter of your torn wedding gown. Bridget let it be known what had happened to your lovely white marriage dress. And what a pity. It would have made a lovely heirloom.' He moved toward the door, glancing back at Patrick and me, who huddled in the shadow of the hideous bronze bull. 'I'm certain that I shall make a far more impressive Count than Bren has been, once he has been removed for

220

his crimes. Thank God you are still alive, dear sister, to testify. And little Patrick there, who, whatever else he might be, happens to be my cousin.'

'Then you don't mean to harm us?' I asked, through the throbbing confusion that felt like something monstrous and alive pressing rhythmically against my brain.

'Quite the contrary, my dear. I have brought you here where you shall be quite safe while I go to rescue poor Maeve. She has had a slight accident, as you know. Quite an ordinary occurrence on Inish Laoghaire, it seems.'

Had whoever had abducted me from the castle, and carried me away on the back of a horse, come upon Maeve? Was that why she had cried out in the darkness, somewhere nearby? The thoughts left me dazed.

Padraic disappeared from the room, with a little backward wave of his white hand pulling the door closed on Patrick and me. I heard the bolt slip into place.

CHAPTER TWENTY-SIX

The glass eyes of the wax figures seemed to be watching us. I sat holding Patrick and tried not to see the graphic display about us as I searched frantically for some route of escape. A privy chamber, I thought, glancing about at the stone walls. The faint tinkle of the stream running beneath the castle came to me from somewhere below the cold floor.

'I don't like him,' Patrick muttered against me. 'I don't like Padraic. Sure the King is best, even if he does hurt people—kill them with his steeplechasers.'

'Darling, maybe it wasn't the King at all,' I said, smoothing his dark head. 'I don't like Padraic either. He could easily have dressed up like the King and worn the shiny boots.'

'He's afraid of horses,' Patrick insisted. 'I saw him running from the King one day. The King was after running Padraic down with his steeplechaser. And then suddenly, the King stopped chasing him, and got down from his horse, and the two were after being good friends again.'

'Maybe you only dreamed it, darling,' I said. 'Yes, I'm certain that it was only a dream.'

I held Patrick close, wondering again whose child he was. Bren's? Had Bren had an affair with Maeve? Or Tim? I had seen the two of them together and had sensed an intimacy between them.

Mercifully, Patrick dozed off, and I sat quietly, lost in a maze of dark, frightening thoughts. Quite against my will, I found myself studying the torture instruments.

A bulky-looking contraption, with a huge posed blade, stood at one side of the bronze bull. I knew immediately that it was a guillotine.

It occurred to me that Padraic was a man of extreme contrasts. His love for flowers and beauty veiled the dark vein of evil flowing beneath his rosy, male attractiveness.

And Bren, who was fierce and savage on the surface—what was beneath all of that rough, rugged maleness? Was he as vicious as he sometimes seemed?

A sound carried through the heavy door. I guessed that Padraic had returned with Maeve. A moment later, he flung open the door to the torture room. Patrick started up at the sound and rubbed his eyes with the back of his hand.

'You may come out now, Deirdre,' Padraic said. 'Join my aunt and me here in my luxurious sitting room, which, you must admit, is much finer than the quarters provided for you by my penurious brother.'

I ignored his remark as I brushed past him, with Patrick still clinging to me.

Maeve lay back on one of the lavish couches; her face was as white as the robe which fell about her body in generous folds.

'You shall remain here while I go to see what is keeping Bren and Dr. Riordan,' Padraic stated.

Puzzled, I noticed that he suddenly avoided looking at me.

'Coward!' Maeve hissed, looking up at him with suddenly malevolent eyes.

'Admittedly, dear Aunt,' Padraic said.

'However, I am certain that you shall manage very well here alone.' He hesitated for an instant, his hand on the door.

'Good-bye, darling Deirdre,' he said, in his strange, hollow voice. He left us then.

Uneasily, I turned to Maeve. 'Is there anything I can do?' I asked.

'That is very kind of you, Deirdre,' she said in her rich, low voice.

I saw that she was herself again; whatever madness had possessed her, earlier, when Patrick and I came upon her, lying injured against the stone fence, had passed. I guessed that it had been the pain from her injury that had brought the legend vividly alive for her. Very gently, I lifted the hem of her robe—then shrunk back appalled. Beneath the purity of her voluminous white garb, Maeve wore shining, black riding boots, identical to those worn by Bren. Above them, I glimpsed the unmistakable flare of dark jodhpurs.

Maeve, then, was the murderer.

'Eileen Maguire,' she said, in her husky, low voice. 'You know of course that you must die. I knew, when you returned, that Padraic had failed me. The fool! He told me that he had taken care of you . . .' She attempted to stand, and broke off with a little groan.

'Twice, he has failed me,' she continued. 'When I fell there on the path and twisted my leg, he said that he would complete the task I had begun. After I had accomplished the worst

224

of it; lured you from your room; carried you down that infernal, slime-riddled ladder of pipes inside the old latrine; and strapped you to the back of the steeplechaser, one of Bren's favorites—Moongold. Spirited beast! Something startled him. He nudged me down onto the stones. Struck out at me with his hoof. There was nothing to do then but to entrust your demise to my nephew. And now he has once more proved himself to be a spineless coward. But perhaps this way is best. This way I shall know that you are dead. Padraic was in love with you, the fool! However, I find that a paltry excuse for cowardice.'

'I can't imagine Padraic loving anyone,' I said, in a remarkably calm voice. 'Not even Eileen Maguire.'

'They were taken in by your soft, sweet ways, the fools. All of them. John. Padraic. Even Bren, who was only a small child. I thought that I had convinced Padraic that none of this could ever belong to him—to *us*; the two of us together—if you were allowed to live and to marry John.' Maeve raised herself up and leaned toward me. 'I killed my own sister to have him,' she said. 'I was only a child, when she married him—the handsome Count O'Leary, King of this island, Lord of this small realm. I loved him from the beginning, more than my sister ever could, even though she bore him his first son. Padraic. He was born seven months after we came here. John

225

wondered about that. I told him that my sister had been wild. And then I waited for him to turn from her and to notice me. I made certain that he would.' Maeve's voice rose triumphantly.

'He did, of course. And made love to me. We were lovers, John and I, before I was sixteen! There was nothing to do then, but to get rid of my sister, so that he might be free to marry me. I pushed her down the stairs. And then . . . I asked him to marry me.'

Suddenly, Maeve's face crumpled.

'But he wouldn't,' she cried. 'And so I killed the others. I killed them all. Mary. Yes, that was the next one's name. Mary O'Leary. She was warming herself before the fire in her gown. I remember that it was made of outing. I had read somewhere that outing is quite explosive when it is new and soft. It was a simple matter to ignite her. A little push. I ran from the room. No one ever guessed.' Maeve's eyes gleamed with the hideous memory.

I cowered before her, holding Patrick to me and trying to shield his small ears from her wild outpouring.

'The one who followed her . . . Found her on the mainland, he did—a petite little thing, named Biddie. A peasant! Mediocre! I was twice the woman that she was. As tall as John. He could never quite grow accustomed to my size. Some men resent largeness in a woman. However, I proved again that I was the better person. Poor Biddie. She had a mania about the old latrine. Imagined that odors still lingered there after all of these years. She designed some odd contraption to be installed inside the walls. A dumbwaiter, it was. Well, she was the one who was dumb!' Maeve emitted a hideous, mirthless laugh.

'I pushed her, one day,' she went on. 'Everyone knew how obsessed she had become about making improvements in the old privy chambers. Several of the servants had remarked that she would one day fall to her death if she persisted in crawling about those dreary privy rooms with her tape measures.'

'And you pushed her,' I said, in a horrified voice.

'Aye, dearie!' Maeve said. 'What else could I have done?' She looked at Patrick, who clung to me, burying his small face in the folds of my skirt. 'Ah, little Bren. His mother was the next,' she said. 'She died in her bed. What could have seemed more natural? It was a simple matter to maintain a condition of sepsis when I attended her in the wee hours of the night. I am very well-informed, my dear Eileen.' She flashed me a quick, taunting look. 'My knowledge of the extraordinary has served me well, as you can see. It was a simple matter to contaminate my hands and the cloths and pads that I used to attend to Nora's needs. That was her name. Nora O'Leary. Odd that I should remember their names when I felt nothing but loathing toward them all for having taken John from me. He wanted no part of me, while he had them. Cast me aside, he did, as though I were an old shoe. Then, when they died, one by one, he came crawling to me with his man-needs, like a dog!' She gave a bitter laugh.

'You!' She pointed an accusing finger at me. 'Eileen Maguire! You were to be his next bride!'

'She was my mother,' I said. 'You are confusing us!'

She seemed not to hear me.

'I intended to see you dead that day on the cliff. I followed you there!' she shouted at me. 'Ah, I remember well how it was. Bren was ill that day with some childhood disease. And you had gone to gather some small treasures to amuse him. I found you there near the bog at the far end of the island; you were squatting on the ledge above the sea, intent on gathering up a nest of gulls' eggs. It would have been a simple matter to push you into those angry waves below.'

'Why didn't you?' I asked, my heart thudding with terror that mingled with a sudden fevered excitement.

'I glanced up, and there was John and your mother. Mrs. Maguire. I think she had become suspicious of me and had talked him into following. The meddling old fool! It was a fine day, and you could see Kilmara there in the distance. I tried to draw back and to pretend that I was admiring the view—that I had leaned over you, only to comment on the little clutch of eggs you had found for Bren. However, I was compelled. I found myself lurching against you, in spite of the danger their presence there presented. But you were stronger than I had anticipated. Little bitch, you fought me like the sly fox you are. You were like a sheep, there on the face of the cliff, darting off from me, so surefooted. I remember how you ran.' Maeve closed her eyes, suddenly, and her face contorted.

'I fell,' she said. 'And suddenly there was John bending over me. I shall never forget the expression that was on his face. One of loathing. Hatred. I knew then how dismally I had failed—that he could never belong to me. I . . . I pushed him with all of my strength. He tumbled downward onto the stones at the base of the headland and hung there, like a child's rag toy. Even from that distance, I could see the great bleeding gash on his head. And the old woman. Mrs. Maguire. She . . . she had fallen, too, even before I struck out at John. I thought that both of them were dead.'

'And Eileen,' I said. 'She must have seen all of it, and thought that they were dead, too. That explains why she left the island—left her mother.'

'Do you take me for a fool?' Maeve shouted at me. 'You are Eileen. I shall never forget the way you stood there above me, watching, your face as white as death. "You've killed them," you screamed down at me over and over again. And then you began to run. I tried to follow, but you had disappeared into one of the caves. There was nothing to do but to take Padraic into my confidence. He had spent a good deal of his time roaming about the island and knew all of the places where you might be hiding.' Maeve flashed an accusing finger at me. 'You had bewitched him, too, with your sickly soft ways! When he returned, he told me that he had destroyed you. He swore that he had thrown you to the sharks! That you were dead!'

'Somehow my mother escaped,' I said. 'It was my mother. You must understand that!'

To convince Maeve that I was not Eileen Maguire loomed in my mind as the only possible way that I might save myself and Patrick. I realized that I was almost begging this madwoman, with her wildly accusing eyes.

' "Returned at last, my Eevelleen," ' Maeve suddenly chanted in the same soft, husky tones that had haunted me from the depths of the castle and on the island ridge. ' "To Dunleary's shore, in answer to the black gull's keen, before death's yielding door." '

'This time, you shan't escape,' she added, ominously.

Patrick looked up at me, white-faced. 'Deirdre, I'm afraid,' he whispered.

'I know, darling,' I said.

I read the hatred and madness in Maeve's eyes, and I knew I had to keep her talking about the past.

I said: 'Katsy. Katsy de Gomez. You killed her, too.'

Before she could reply, a key grated in the lock, and the door opened.

I turned quickly toward it; Bren's name was on my lips.

Padraic stood there, locking the door carefully behind him. He turned to give me a surprised look.

'You're still here,' he said, with a lift of his burnished brows. He turned to Maeve. 'I should have thought that you would have completed your grisly task by now,' he said. Then, in a low, tense voice. 'They've come. Bren and Dr. Riordan. Tim Donahue is with them. And the legless old fisherman. Pat Mor.'

'Pat Mor?' Maeve gave him a questioning look.

'The old man with the glass. Mrs. Maguire's ancient paramour. No doubt he has come to join the wake.'

Padraic turned to Patrick and me. There was no mistaking the fear in his eyes.

'Sorry, dear sister,' he said. 'I must ask you to step back into the torture chamber. I've no choice. I do hope that you understand.' He gave a nervous shrug. 'What a pity that Bren happened onto your charming photo in that

231

newspaper. Odd how fate works. I'd no idea that Eileen swam so well. I still can't imagine how she managed to reach the mainland. In a rather obscure way, I'm glad. I really was quite fond of the girl, you know. However, living on an island swarming with black-visaged O'Learys, my dear, I hadn't a chance. It seems that she preferred the old Count, even though he was twice her age, and Bren, who was a wet-nosed urchin at the time.' Padraic came near to me. 'I have never quite overcome the passion I had for her. I realized that the instant I laid eyes on you. Her rejection of me was a terrible blow to my pride.'

'Your pride!' I gasped, stepping backward, in an effort to escape Padraic's outreaching arms.

My shoulder grazed against the torture room door.

'You've no idea, my dear, what a blow it can be to a man's ego, when he is in the process of making love to a woman, to have her suddenly wrench herself away.' Padraic advanced on me, and I backed into the torture chamber, suddenly oblivious to its horrendous instruments.

'No!' I cried.

Beyond his shoulder, I glimpsed Patrick, crying and huddled in a corner of one of the lavish couches, and Maeve's face, twisted with a terrible malevolence.

'Please,' I begged. 'We can talk about it

sometime. But not now. Not here. Not with a child watching.'

'But I insist, my darling,' Padraic said. 'I am quite willing to let you live. Indeed, I have done that—left you there on the path, for Tim to find. I heard him coming.'

'Coward!' Maeve hissed, behind us.

Padraic ignored her.

'If you promise to make it well worth my while, darling, we have only to rid ourselves of that venomous bitch, Maeve. Blame her death on Bren. Darling Deirdre. Don't you see, you've aroused all of the old desire—desires that Eileen only laughed at! Scorned! You can't know what it has been like, living here on this barren island, where there are no desirable women. Only whores, like that black little bitch who followed me from Spain, determined to retrieve her priceless relics. If it had not been for Bren, she and I might have . . . But never mind that. It is quite another story. And there is Maeve, of course—the prize whore of them all.'

Maeve emitted an inhuman cry.

'How dare you?' she screamed at Padraic. 'How dare you speak of me in such a manner? As though *she* were the only virgin—the only one who is innocent and pure. Eileen Maguire! How I loathe her smug virtues. You!' She pointed a venomous finger at me. 'You, with your white wedding dress and your sickly sweet ways! Taking them all in, even Tim

233

Donahue, who had the audacity to tell me how lucky he considered The O'Leary, to have found for himself a decent woman. And Bren . . .' Maeve arose from the couch and hobbled toward us, forgetting her injured ankle. 'That's right, dearie.' As she thrust her face toward me, the flesh twisted about her mouth in a violent contortion and made her seem suddenly old. 'Your precious little Bren. He's a man, now. He needed a woman, the same as the rest of them on this cursed island. Then she came, that black Spanish bitch, and he grew keen for her wiles.' Maeve threw her head back, and laughed jarringly.

'I warned him against her! But he had to discover for himself what she was! She could think of nothing but her precious antiques and Captain de Medina's gold. She knew that it was hidden here somewhere, waiting all of these years, she said, for a De Medina to return to this cursed place and claim it. She had read of it somewhere in Juan de Medina's log. She took pride in the fact that she was a member of his family, just as you, Eileen Maguire, had prided yourself on your innocence! She had it all planned; marry The O'Leary and become the Countess, which entitled her to a share of his wealth.' Maeve turned suddenly to Padraic. 'How much did that black bitch offer you, nephew, to relinquish her precious family treasures? Herself, of course, and a goodly portion from the O'Leary coffers, I can well imagine!'

Padraic stared at his aunt. 'How did you know?' he asked.

'Like Patrick, I know everything that happens on this island,' Maeve said. 'I'm sure that you understand now, Padraic, why I had to be rid of her, as I had to rid myself of the others.'

'I understand that you are the prize madame on this island, and that you intend to keep it that way,' Padraic said. 'However, dear Aunt, even you must realize by now that no one—not the old Count or anyone else—is about to ask for your hand in marriage. How many times have you been rejected during these past years? And now that you are growing old . . .' Padraic shrugged.

'You know that I have not been free to accept proposals,' Maeve cried. 'Even if the old Count had wanted me, I should have had to turn him down! Juan. Juan de Medina is returning to marry me! He should be arriving any day now, to claim me, his darling Maeve!'

'Solace yourself with your pure robes and your mad thoughts of Captain de Medina, if you will, poor Maeve,' Padraic said. 'How comforting it must be to you to play the perpetual ingenue, awaiting her white knight! However, the harsh fact remains that you are inescapably a whore.'

He turned once more to me, dismissing Maeve with a cold shrug.

235

Suddenly, she flew at him, screaming, and the two of them stumbled backward, grappling and tearing at each other. Maeve's hair, which had flowed free from its braid, swayed and twined about them, like slim crimson snakes. I thought of the Gorgon, Medusa. This is some hideous nightmare, I told myself. It can't be real.

Suddenly, their feet entrapped by Maeve's flowing robe, the struggling figures stumbled against the guillotine. Padraic bent Maeve's tall body backward beneath the blade, hovering over her like some black-garbed executioner from the past.

I stared at the quivering blade above them.

Then as it plunged downward, I screamed, and dashed from the room, slamming the door quickly behind me.

CHAPTER TWENTY-SEVEN

It is difficult for me to remember what happened next. I recall holding Patrick close and the two of us comforting each other as best we could.

There was no sound from the torture chamber, and I remember thinking that I must steel myself to go search Padraic's person for a key. The idea seemed quite remote; my taxed mind could not admit that there was any reality behind that closed door.

'I want to go,' Patrick said, against me. 'I want to go home.'

'Soon. darling. Soon. We must wait for Bren. Surely he has a key.'

'The King?' Patrick said. 'Sure I saw his trousers beneath *her* white dress. And the boots. The shiny boots.'

'She was sick, darling. Terribly sick,' I said.

'She is after being in there dead, then?' Patrick gestured toward the locked door. 'The two of them? Are they both dead now?'

'I don't know,' I said, avoiding looking at the door.

I noticed the wadded blanket that had supported Maeve when Patrick and I came upon her on the island ridge. It had fallen open, and a dark, man's cap spilled from its folds. There was a jacket, as well, like the jacket Bren wore, when he rode; this was the remainder of Maeve's disguise. Somehow, she had managed to exchange the jacket for her robe as she lay nursing her wounded ankle, waiting for Padraic to return and tell her that he had tossed me into the sea.

When my headache eased, I told myself, I would search for a key. I forced myself to look at the torture chamber door, trying not to imagine what lay behind it. Then suddenly, the door began to inch open. I pressed Patrick's dark head against my breast, staring at it in horrified fascination.

A man emerged. I realized that it was Bren, white-faced, his eyes filled with dread. Faintly, I heard someone crying his name. Later, I learned that it had been me.

*   *   *

I awoke in the high bed that I shared with Bren. Patrick sat nearby on a tall chair.

'He said I could stay,' Patrick told me.

I reached to take his hand.

'Who said, darling?' I asked, trying to remember.

'The King,' Patrick said. 'And Dr. Riordan. He gave you a shot, with a needle and you slept. He gave me one, as well. Sure and I awoke first, and came to find you, and he was after saying that I could stay, if I would be very quiet.'

Then suddenly there was Bren coming toward me, his face fierce with some deep emotion.

I thought: This is my husband. The veil of suspicion through which I had regarded him since the death of my cousin had suddenly lifted, without my realizing it. It was as though I were seeing him clearly, for the first time. The guarded fierceness in his face wasn't really a fierceness at all, but a savage and consuming desire to protect me from the dark shadows that lurked on Inish Laoghaire.

He spoke my name, and we clung together

for a long while.

Then because Bren was with me, I dared to remember.

CHAPTER TWENTY-EIGHT

A year has passed since Padraic and Maeve died together in the torture chamber. But I still recall the events of that night with a sense of horror.

When I asked Bren the following day, how he had found Patrick and me in the depths of the old castle, he told me that he had climbed down through the maze of pipes inside of Dunleary's walls.

'But I looked for a privy chamber in Padraic's rooms, hoping that we might somehow escape,' I said. 'There seemed to be none.'

'Padraic had disguised it behind one of those ugly machines,' Bren said. 'I suppose it gave him a sense of security. It was a simple matter for me to shove it aside once I had discovered that Padraic was involved in your disappearance and had found my way down to his private realm, hoping to take him by surprise.'

'Who told you that Padraic was involved? Or did you guess?' I asked.

'Pat Mor. Although I was suspicious of

Padraic all along. Pat Mor saw Maeve murder Mrs. Maguire through his glass. Your grandmother, darling.' He pulled me tight, and said in a soft, tender voice, 'You did know about her?'

I nodded.

'Pat saw Maeve smother her, and Padraic lurking there in the shadows, looking on. Pat had seen a good many things through the years, and suddenly he realized what they meant. He insisted on coming to the island with Dr. Riordan and me. He told me everything. How Padraic tried to make love to Eileen the day she ran away from here. Pat thought at the time that there was a clandestine romance between the two of them. Pat had seen Eileen often on the sea cliffs, with Padraic nearby, slipping about as though he had arranged to meet her somewhere away from the castle.' Bren paused, his eyes growing thoughtful. 'I can remember times when I was with her, that she seemed frightened. I think that she knew Padraic was about, spying on her. At any rate, it was no surprise to Pat Mor to see them together, that day, in the cave, where she had run to hide from Maeve.

'Then, when Eileen wrenched free of Padraic's abrupt advances, and dove into the sea, Pat Mor assumed that the two of them had quarrelled—that she was playing the tease, daring Padraic to follow her into the cold water.' Bren's face was grim, as he spoke.

A rap on the door interrupted him. He called out, and a man entered our room, rolling himself along on a cart. I saw at once that he had no legs, and knew that this was Pat Mor, the man with the glass.

'Sure I've come to offer the young Countess me condolences,' he said. 'Your grandmother was a fine woman, and her daughter, Eileen, as well. Ach, I curse myself over and over again for having been suspicious of the girl. I assumed that she was only after codding Padraic that day, in the little cave, when what the poor girl was doing was attempting to escape his lewd attempts to seduce her. Sure I was influenced by the legend, the same as the rest. God's grace, what would ye have had me to think, under the circumstances?' The old man's eyes grew vague. 'She carried off a little packet with her, when she ran from him and leapt into the sea. Sure he has given her some bright bauble, I thought, and her, refusing him, now she has it in her hands.'

'It was the book of poetry,' Bren said. 'The one I had stolen from Father's room. I couldn't write verse to her, as he did. Yet, I wanted to give her something. I loved her, as only a small boy can love an older woman. I remember picking a small bouquet of bog cotton tassels to tuck into it. That pitiful little cluster of flowers pressed between the pages of Father's book was my contribution to the wooing of Eileen Maguire . . .'

241

'She kept them for as long as she lived,' I said. 'She must have loved both of you very much.'

'I saw her with Tim Donahue, later that day, rowing across to the mainland in a curragh,' Pat Mor said. 'And myself after thinking that it was for her wedding finery that she was coming ashore.'

'She never returned to Inish Laoghaire,' Bren said.

'I'm after knowing how wrong I was now,' Pat Mor said, looking up at us with eyes pleading for understanding. 'It took the death of that fine woman at the hands of that wicked banshee to bring me to my senses.'

And so, at last, I knew the secret of my mother's past.

There was no need for Pat Mor to tell us that he had seen Maeve with Tim and Padraic, and a number of the village men, or that he knew a good deal about Katsy de Gomez, who had, for a short time, been Bren's wife.

Because my vision had grown remarkably clear, I knew how Bren had felt about Katsy; he had been betrayed, his pride miserably shattered, even though his attraction to her had been shallow—the passion of a man deprived. I guessed how much more attractive the dark-haired, Spanish girl must have seemed to him than Maeve, and although it pained me to think that he hadn't trusted me with the truth about his past, I felt that I understood. I remembered those times when he had seemed on the verge of revealing some dark secret to me, and, knowing that he had tried, was comforted.

There still remained the secret of Patrick's parentage. It was, I thought, almost too painfully obvious, as I watched Patrick with Bren, that there was a close relationship between the two of them. Their brows soared at the same devilish angle, and even the bright dancing lights that flickered in their eyes were the same.

*   *   *

Pat Mor stayed on at Dunleary for my grandmother's funeral. On that day, he came to me. I was alone in the castle dining room arranging silver for the meal which was to be served to the mourners who had come up from the village to join the wake. Bren was with his steeplechasers. The two of us were alone.

'I've been after seeing more than I should,' Pat Mor said. 'Ach, the way ye look from one to the other of them, and back again, when the three of ye are together now.'

Patrick spent a good deal of time at the castle, now, and I knew at once what the old man meant.

'It is after thinking that ye should have the full truth of the matter, I am,' he continued, looking up at me from his low-wheeled cart.

'Sure it is a fine boy, he is, and it is only right that the world should know whose gossoon he be.'

'No!' I protested sharply. 'Really. It can make no possible difference.'

'Ye wouldn't be frightened now, would ye— a fine, brave young woman like yerself,' Pat Mor said. 'There is no reason for it. It is after being born underneath the blue sky, the little one was, which may be why he's keen for the open air, with no thought of a roof over his head when it pours.' The legless old man's head nodded slowly with recollection.

I turned from him, busying myself with the heavy old silver, which bore the intricate imprint of the O'Leary arms. There were lists to be checked off for the servants. I tried to shut out his flow of words, but I found myself listening to his narrative, almost against my will.

'The gossoon's father was there at the time—the only one, I'm thinking, who knew. I watched the two of them through me glass. She was straining like an animal to expel the child, giving birth there in the little croft, near the bog, the blood staining her white robe. He had brought a blanket for her to wrap the newborn in. Sure I knew, watching them, that they had arranged it all together. The robes she always wore were after guarding her guilty secret. No one guessed now how it was with her, she being a woman well past her prime.

244

Who but the devil himself would have suspected it? It was himself who carried the infant off, and left it on Sheila O'Leary's doorstep to be reared as her own. Sheila had gone off to the bog that day, to catch the turf for Tim, and the child was there when the two of them returned.'

'Sheila thought the child was Tim's,' I said. 'I hoped that he was.'

But Tim had been there with his mother in the bog, I thought, while Patrick was being born. It couldn't have been Tim. I busied myself with a pencil, marking off my list.

Behind me, Pat Mor said, in a voice remarkably soft and kind: 'Sure it was the old Count, Roisin. I'd not want ye to be thinking any different. It was he who carried the child to his sister's stoop, and left him there to be found. God's grace, where else could he have taken him?'

I turned suddenly and bent to kiss the grizzled old man, squatted there on his little wheeled cart.

'Ach, Roisin,' he said. 'Sure I thought you should know.'

*   *   *

They no longer speak of the curse on the mainland, or here on Inish Laoghaire. For when the final reckoning was made, no one could remember anything out of the ordinary

245

having happened to O'Leary women in the times before Maeve first came to the island. It was then that the legend had been revived following upon tragic deaths of the old Count's wives. Rumors of their unfaithfulness were traced, by the village men, directly to Maeve, who had entertained most of them, on occasion, with tales of the strange happenings up at the castle, as well as with her charms. There can be no doubt that she was affected more strongly than any of us, by the legend, with its dire curse. Poor Maeve. Her white knight never came to claim her.

There was only the gold, hidden in the Spanish Cave on Maguire Island. My island, now. Mine and Bren's. We are both agreed that it is actually only an extension of Inish Laoghaire. Its value is purely sentimental. There is nothing there now, save the remains of an ancient stone cottage where the Maguires had lived for hundreds of years.

It was Bren's wish to turn what remained of Captain Juan de Medina's treasure, as well as Padraic's grisly collection, over to the state. The Spaniards as well are gone; their remains have been removed by the handsome young Irishmen sent by the government to lift the rotted chests from the old moldering galleon.

There are only the Irish here now. We O'Learys. Bren still carries a frayed clipping from the *San Francisco Chronicle* in his pocket, and the two of us often marvel together over the strange workings of fate.

It had been his intention, once he had traced my background, to bring me back with him to Inish Laoghaire for my grandmother's sake.

As Bren told me: 'I knew that Eileen hadn't died here on the island. We all knew. A thousand nostalgic memories flooded over me, the instant I saw the photograph of you in the *Chronicle*. I was suddenly a child again, roaming about the island with a charming freckle-faced woman, who made me feel very loved and secure. I knew at once that I must find you. Bring you back here. I suppose I had some vague notion that you would be like her. Like Eileen. You must know, darling, that she was like a mother to me.

'Then when I saw you standing there, beneath the Yacht Club arch, with your little cluster of roses clutched timidly in your hand, I was suddenly a man gazing upon a delightful young woman, blossoming, but not quite full-blown . . . Now I am sounding like the old Count, and I don't mean to. But your innocence that night was so obvious. I was almost afraid to bring you to this place, riddled as it was by vile deeds. Yet I knew that I must—not for your grandmother's sake alone, but for my own. And Eileen's, too, I suppose. It seemed to be where you truly belonged. I had an odd feeling that I would be making it up to her by bringing you back to this island that she loved. Deirdre the virgin,' he added, the mischief that I loved, coming over him. 'That was before I realized how much I loved you.'

I confessed to Bren all of the doubts I had had and now, when we stand looking out over our islands—Inish Laoghaire and Maguire Island beyond, in all of its barren but dignified beauty—Bren teases me sometimes because I suspected him of marrying me for the island.

We laugh, then, and Bren reminds me of my wifely duties; now that Maguire Island is in the family, he expects a dozen sons.

Often, I recall my mother's words: 'He has the worst as well as the best of the Irish in him,' and I am amazed at how much it pleases me to see Bren in that particular light.

I think of the years ahead—the years of growth and mutual discovery, with all of their rich promise—and suddenly the old castle seems very cozy and bright, and I am content.